The Sleepless

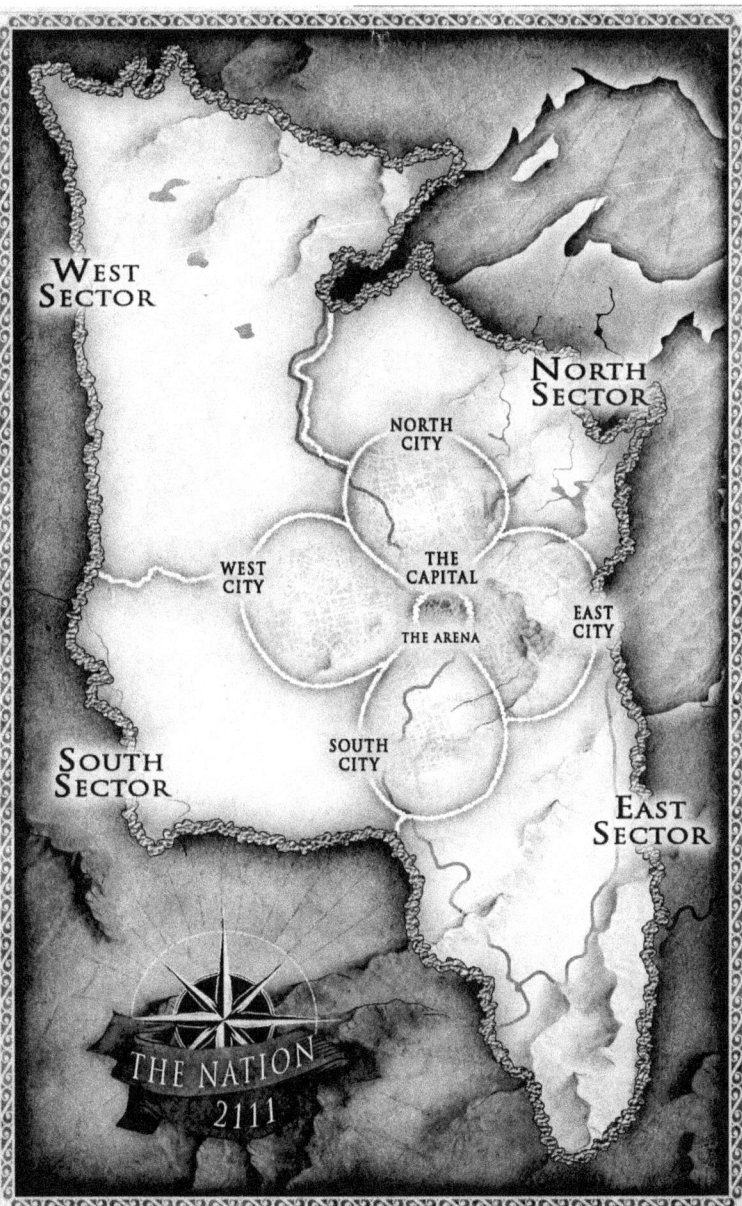

WEST
SECTOR

NORTH
SECTOR

NORTH
CITY

WEST
CITY

THE
CAPITAL

EAST
CITY

THE ARENA

SOUTH
SECTOR

SOUTH
CITY

EAST
SECTOR

THE NATION
2111

The Sleepless

Insomnolence: Book 1

D.K. Cassidy

ISBN: 978-1-941938-04-1
Library of Congress Control Number: 2017938510

Editing: Crystal Watanabe
Cover Design: Artie Cabrera
Interior Design: Polgarus Studio

To Mark, Aidan, Jared, Nikko,
Moongie, Bubbles, and Mochi.

Chapter 1

January 23, 2101

D r. Annie Beaumont left the meeting with her manager feeling conflicted. She had been given access to a secret project at the Centers for Disease Control and wanted to wipe everything she'd read from her memory. Phrases like 'biological warfare' and 'secret testing' made her nervous. In all her years employed at the CDC, she'd worked on what she considered good projects. Trying to find the cure for diseases, or tracking the source of a contamination incident.

Annie considered her position as an epidemiologist a source of pride. She began there as a medical officer, testing research by others, investigating and analyzing the data given to her. After a few years of what she viewed as desk work, she applied for a new position and was hired as an epidemiologist. Being part of the actual research turned out to be a better fit for her ability and temperament.

The project had begun six months earlier, but Annie wasn't allowed in until her security clearance was raised to 'Top Secret.' Then, instead of developing vaccines and antidotes, she was instructed to begin the development of a virus. One that could, and most likely would, be used against the enemies of the United States. The barbaric request was cloaked in patriotism, as most requests like it were.

Riding the train home, she wondered if her husband could be trusted with the information. She wanted to talk about her new assignment with someone. In the past he had been her sounding board. Annie missed those days. His security clearance was high enough, but there was something different about him now. The change began after the State Department sent him on a trip to Russia. When he returned, he couldn't meet her eyes or talk to her for longer than a couple of minutes without needing to leave the room. Before his trip, they'd spend their evenings discussing their projects. She was a scientist; he was a diplomat.

His relationship with their daughter, Larissa, wasn't the same, either. Annie knew that four-year-old Larissa couldn't understand why Daddy no longer wanted to play. Each time he said, "Daddy is busy now," Annie's heart broke.

"Jared, I think it's time we talk. You've been avoiding me and Larissa since you returned from your last trip, and I want—no, I *need* to know why."

Jared seemed oddly panicked, trying not to look at Annie. This time Annie was determined to find out what the problem might be. She grabbed both sides of his face and turned his head so he couldn't avoid her gaze.

"I mean it, Jared. Tell me now."

She could hear the desperation in her voice, and she found herself hoping he could as well.

"I... well, I can't. They won't let me. You're better off this way. Seriously, Annie. I've never kept a secret from you, but this is different."

"But who is 'they,' Jared? Please don't shut me out."

"Don't make this hard on me, Annie. I'm doing what's best for all of us. I was going to tell you this later, but I might as well get it over with."

She stopped and stared at him, afraid of the words she already knew would come out of his mouth.

"I'm going on another trip," he said, "and this time I'll be gone for a few months."

September 6, 2101, eight months later.

She tossed and turned the entire evening, unable to sleep. She tried taking one of the sleeping pills her doctor had prescribed for occasional insomnia. It did nothing. Kate wondered if the tablets were expired. She got out of bed and turned on the light to read the bottle. Nope. The pills were still good. Warm milk sometimes helped, so Kate went to her kitchen and microwaved a mug of milk and honey. The comforting steam from the mug relaxed her but still didn't bring on sleep. At last she climbed into her bed, hoping that if she laid still, she'd at last go to sleep.

Kate left her bed the next morning grumbling about having to go to work. She hadn't slept the previous night, unable to get comfortable or turn off her thoughts. Her cat, Moongie, kept licking her face and waking her up with unexplained urgency. Looking back, Kate knew Moongie was aware of the change. A change that would affect her and everyone that she knew.

A week later, sirens sounded throughout the city while people from the CDC, dressed in anti-contamination suits, knocked on doors and yelled through megaphones, ordering everyone to evacuate.

A new reality began that day for Kate and thousands of others like her.

Chapter 2

February 9, 2111
10 Years AIB

The last time she slept was three days ago, and she was feeling desperate. She'd checked her sleep card—or what everyone called their SC—one week ago and thought she'd banked more than enough hours to get her through the weekend. She trusted the information, never thinking it might be wrong. Her SC meant life.

There'd been an upgrade to the main server, and some citizens had their accounts messed up—she was one of them. Lucky her. An incorrect overage of twenty-four hours had given her a false sense of security. She'd thought she could put off earning credits for a few more days, which was fine with her. Kate had wanted a few days alone.

Wrong.

Today she wished she had the connections necessary to get a regular job. One that involved nothing distasteful or physical. She could imagine herself working in the Capitol Building, answering emails, organizing meetings, anything to keep her away from the list of tasks she was expected to perform. Reconsidering that option, she knew being that close to the government wouldn't be good for her. She'd spend her time there resenting the President and possibly getting arrested for saying the wrong thing. Better to stay where she was in North City.

She'd even become a farmer, even though she'd killed all her houseplants in her previous home. Not on purpose; she didn't have a green thumb. That didn't seem to matter for the farmers, who grew crops using tractors and automatic seeding machines. They set the sprinklers and waited for the crops to grow. Everything was on a precise schedule, foolproof farming. Once, she asked about what the farmers grew. The overseers at the farm told her to mind her own business; there were no jobs for her. What that meant was she didn't know the right people to get her on the list to work there.

Her parents died years ago, and her only living relative, her grandmother, Bridget, disappeared only a few hours AIB. Kate had searched the list of deceased compiled by the government and didn't see her grandmother's name. Hoping Bridget was still alive but thinking the chance was next to nil, Kate tried to remember the good times with her grandmother. She'd given up searching for Bridget years ago.

No one mentioned the unintentionally cute acronym for the time prior, BIB, Before Insomnolence Began, in public. AIB, After Insomnolence Began, was the only way to mark dates now. The official calendar said it was 10, but she insisted on keeping track of the years in the old way. To her, it was 2111.

She kept this bit of rebellion to herself.

Stumbling to the assignments window to receive her next job, she shoved her SC toward the clerk and waited.

"Looks like you need to earn credits in a hurry."

"Nothing like stating the obvious!" Kate said.

"Look, Katie, if you want me to give you a job, you'd better be nicer to me."

"Hey, my name's not Katie. I changed it years ago. It's Kate, not that it matters to you, I suppose."

She tried to control her temper, but it was hard; Kate had to correct the clerks every time she went to any of them for jobs. What they called her wasn't the point. Maintaining control over some aspect of her life mattered to her. This clerk, Pete, had the power to refuse her a job, and a reputation for being one of the nasty guys. Without access to work she'd die. It was simple: no work equals no sleep equals death. She knew a human could only last between one to two weeks without sleeping. Kate needed to keep her temper under control and stop letting this creep get to her.

Pete tapped Kate's gateway to slumber on the metal counter, considering which of the tasks to assign to her. Kate could tell desperation excited him, which was why he made her wait a few more seconds.

"Here, everything you need to know is on this flash drive. Next!"

"Thank you, I'm sorry I snapped. I'm not usually so cranky, but I really need to—"

"Get out of line now or I'll take back the assignment!" Pete yelled, exposing a mouthful of dark, twisted teeth. "Next!"

Kate hurried away from the window, cradling the black flash drive. It was her salvation and her torment. Not able to go far without wasting energy, she moved to the corner of the Great Hall.

The Great Hall served as a gathering place for citizens and a spot for the bureaucrats to perform functions unnecessary before the nightmare started. In the past, the building was used as a bus station, the high ceilings echoing arrivals and departures, hellos and goodbyes. No physical changes were needed to convert it except for a new sign covering the old one—what was once Greyhound now said Great Hall.

Looking for a quiet spot, Kate found a corner of the hall to sit. From her seat she had a view of the Wall—the structure composed of twenty-first-century garbage forming an irregular ring around the Nation. She remembered the rush of near panic when the CDC ordered the area surrounding the infection enclosed. Facing an election year, the Bureau of Fiscal Services thought a grand gesture would ensure their re-election. The winning idea: scrape the leftovers of the survivors' lives into walls.

Refrigerators, furniture, books, anything left behind formed the three-hundred-foot wall, keeping the sleepless contained. There was no way out of the Nation since it was dangerous to go to the wasteland that was once the United States. The sleepless were told they were the last survivors of the plague, and they believed it.

Kate removed her cap and felt the back of her skull for her port. She'd need another haircut soon; her deep auburn hair covered the port, making it much more difficult to use. There was no requirement to keep her hair short, but there was no reason to grow it long, the way she used to wear it. Vanity was dead, replaced with the need for slumber. The flash drive fit into the slot and she began to download her next task.

Cleanup. Damn, she hated those kinds of jobs. Why did she have to suffer due to a glitch on the server? She'd promised herself she'd never do a cleanup again.

That clerk is just punishing me for snapping at him. Jerk! She wouldn't forget this.

The location and details of the task flashed through her head, causing her stomach to churn. After a dozen of these she'd hoped for some level of callousness. No luck. Kate felt her heart racing. At least she still had feelings. For now.

Exhausted but knowing she needed to accomplish her task *today*, she stood up and shuffled toward the ITS, the Intercity Transport Subway. Her focus for now was on moving her feet with as little effort as possible to conserve her energy.

The hall was emptying, everyone heading to their assignments. Kate hoped she'd see her best friend, Decker. Best friend. How funny. He was her only friend, the lone person she trusted. He endured cleanups to help her out, offering to accompany Kate whenever he came into North City.

Kate scanned the crowd, hopeful Decker would turn up. Wishing she could call him but knowing it was impossible. He appeared on his own terms. There was still so much she didn't know about him but couldn't ask. His mysterious life away from her kept her safe, according to Decker. She asked no questions. After a defeated last look around, she headed to the subway station.

Decker was one of the lucky ones. He still slept.

Chapter 3

April 22, 2101
Six months BIB

Sifting through her mail, Kate noticed a handwritten letter addressed to her. Nobody ever sent her letters; nobody sent letters, period. She'd almost tossed the missive, but its thickness caught her attention, and when she read her name, her proper name, Katherine, she was intrigued.

There was no return address on the mystery letter, her address and name written in a loopy cursive with emerald-green ink, the paper a thick ivory vellum. This rated high on the excitement meter for Kate since her current occupation was as a barista at a local independent coffee shop with the less-than-original name of *The Cup*. This was the only job a new college graduate could get with a degree in history.

It was supposed to be a temporary job, but several months later she was getting discouraged trying to find her dream job in a museum. Apparently, history museums had a low attrition rate. Now why hadn't her college career counselor told her that important bit of news?

Before she could think of opening the mystery letter, Kate went to her refrigerator and stared at its contents for a couple of minutes, willing it to be full of tasty treats instead of one bottle of ginger ale and leftovers from three nights ago. She should have taken one of the sandwiches from the coffee shop but couldn't bear the thought of eating one more day-old roast beef sandwich.

It was time to play the grandmother card and pay her a visit. She hopped on her bicycle and rode the three miles to Grandmother Bridget's home. She salivated as she imagined all the food waiting for her in that messy, cozy apartment.

As always, her grandmother somehow knew she was coming and was heating up the chicken and dumplings she'd made earlier in the day.

"Hi, honey, dinner is almost ready. I thought I was wrong about you showing up, but there you are."

"Why won't you tell me how you know when I'm coming over for a visit?"

Bridget gave Kate one of her mysterious smiles.

"I know. Somehow I always know; it's a grandmother's intuition. I can feel you heading in my direction."

Kate sat at the little oilcloth-covered table and traced the pattern of cherries with her forefinger while waiting for her meal. She thought there was a bump in the chair but realized she'd put the letter in the back pocket of her jeans. She used the thick letter as a fan to stave off the heat of the kitchen.

It was time to open it and find out what was going on. She grabbed a steak knife from her grandmother's utensil drawer and slid it under the flap. This was the type of letter that called for a letter opener and not fingers with their ragged nails bitten down.

The first thing Kate noticed about the letter was the brevity of it. She'd been expecting a long tome given the thickness, but it was two pages with a personalized greeting and four sentences on the first page and a map on the second. The first page said:

Salutations, Katherine,

Your time has come. Be a part of a new and better future. With your help we can create a superior product.

It begins on the first Saturday of June 2101, at 5 PM

The second page was a detailed map from her apartment to the brand-new Pippin Corp office building downtown.

Kate was disappointed. In her mind it was spam, and she assumed the same letter had arrived in thousands of mailboxes.

Kate showed the letter to her grandmother.

"Isn't this the strangest thing you've ever seen? A better product? I'm not a techie. What do you think, Grandma?"

"Let me read this one more time."

Bridget reread the letter and looked at the map.

"You're right, this is pretty weird. Toss it. Better yet, just throw it on the fire and forget it ever arrived. I'm sure many people got these letters and some fools will volunteer, but it need not be you. Now, let's eat."

As suggested, Kate tossed it into Bridget's fireplace and ate, listening to her adored grandmother tell her about her ordinary day. There was no green ink, no invitations to curious events, and no mystery. Bridget told her about the latest book group she'd attended, and the beautiful yarn she'd gotten for a steal at the shop down the street. In Kate's world, these were things grandmothers did, nothing cryptic. Just comforting.

"Kate, dear, I need to go to bed. Stay safe going home."

As she cycled home that evening, all thoughts of the letter left her head, a spark blown away by the rush of air passing over her.

By the time she entered her tiny apartment, Kate was thinking about work the next morning, wishing her shift did not begin at 6 AM She was not, and never would be, a morning person. Maybe after a few months she could take the evening shift, but that would mean giving up on finding work in a museum.

No, she decided. She was not giving up. She was just being, as was her tendency, practical. If she continued working at her current job, she should at least have decent hours. Looking at the alarm clock perched on the edge of her nightstand, she was unhappy to see 11 PM on the display.

Ugh, another night short of sleep.

There was no way she could be pleasant to customers when she was so sleep deprived. Trying to keep their orders straight while being exhausted was a going to be a challenge.

When did it become cool to order a coffee that had so many exceptions it sounded like a formula for a complicated chemical compound instead of a beverage? Half caffeine, nonfat, low foam, wet, dry, extra hot, soy, almond milk, two shots, etc., etc., ad nauseam. Didn't anyone order a simple coffee anymore?

Then there was the group that irritated her most: those who came into the coffee shop and ordered nothing that even resembled coffee. Smoothies! Frozen confections that might as well be called milkshakes, but no, they wouldn't sound as hip. Hot chocolate, Italian sodas, milk with flavorings.

She needed to get another job.

Her frustration would kill her if she didn't make a change, and soon. She promised herself that tomorrow she would comb the job sites yet again and maybe even stop by some of the museums in person. It's much more difficult to say no to someone who is standing in front of you. Then at least they could picture her as they went through her resume. Imagine her face as they rejected her.

Enough venting, time to go to bed. It was 11:30 PM, and she had to be up in five and a half hours. *I am definitely a night owl, so why do I work mornings at a coffee shop?*

Moongie, her cat, sensed her frustration and jumped on Kate's lap, purring. Kate calmed down and started to absently scratch her kitty's head. After a few minutes she headed to the bathroom to brush her teeth.

Back in bed, her thoughts drifted back to the strange letter, and she concluded it was a new form of marketing. She couldn't believe a huge company like Pippin Corp hired someone to handwrite letters to potential testers. Or had printing become so sophisticated that the difference between print and handwriting was now indistinguishable?

Thinking about the letter segued into a daydream about her perfect job. She'd studied history because she wanted to work in a museum. Her first choice was the National Museum, but any place that had 'museum' in the name would do for now. She wanted to be a conservator and save precious artifacts that offered a glimpse into past societies.

She imagined herself restoring an illuminated manuscript with care, wearing white gloves while dusting off centuries of dirt, skin flakes, and whatever else made its way onto the beautiful pages.

Or she could see herself being in charge of acquisitions. Jetting around the world looking for treasures and convincing countries to lend their artifacts to her to display in her museum. She smiled at the phrase 'her museum.'

Kate let her mind wander to think about her perfect partner in life. He would need to be interested in history and be willing to lead an unconventional lifestyle. She lied to herself with the thought looks wouldn't be important, but relented and admitted to herself that the guy she wound up with had to be gorgeous. She turned to look at her clock again and was shocked to see it was now 12:30 AM

Ugh. Five hours and another day of coffee for the masses.

April 25, 2101

While cycling home from her shift at The Cup, Kate's phone rang. She let it go to voicemail; no one she knew ever called. If it was important, they'd text her. It wasn't until she reached her apartment that she checked the message.

"Oh my God, it's the history museum!" said Kate to her disinterested cat.

She needed to tell someone and knew it would be Bridget. Riding her bicycle to her grandmother's apartment in record time, she couldn't wait to share her news.

"Grandma! Guess what?"

"Well, hello to you, Kate," Bridget said rather coolly. "Won't you come in?"

"Okay, message received, Grandma. How are you today?"

"Never mind, you seem to be pretty excited about something," said Bridget.

"Only the best news ever! The National History Museum offered me a job! Like an idiot I didn't answer my phone and let it go to voicemail and by the time I got the message they were closed and—"

"Slow down, Kate," her grandmother said with a chuckle. "You can call them tomorrow and accept the job. I'm so proud of you, honey. Your parents would be, too. I wish they were still alive so you could tell them. Come, give me a hug."

They embraced for a few seconds before Kate asked about food. Bridget set the table and dished up the macaroni she'd made.

Chapter 4

Moongie greeted her with more impatience than normal, seeming anxious for her to enter the apartment and get on with her routine. Kate opened a can of cat food, thinking that was what she wanted, but Moongie ignored the food. Her cat wanted to be petted and continued to butt against Kate's legs until her human complied.

Happy to have this particular week behind her, it was nice for her to relax in her cozy apartment. The museum had been crazy for days while they got ready for the new exhibit about World War IV. There were websites to update, blogs to write, and docents to train.

The WWIV exhibition did not draw the crowds that Mythic Creatures had, but the director of the museum told the staff he wanted to go in a different direction and expose the populace to lesser-known events in history. It was her job, besides being a conservator, to make sure everyone in the city knew about the event.

There was not enough money to hire a proper public-relations person, so being the newest member of the staff—and the only one accustomed to using social media—made her the director's first and only choice. Her ever-present smartphone could never be out of reach. She didn't mind; it seemed to be part of her already.

As if on cue, her phone rang.

"Kate, I wanted to check in with you," said the head curator. "How are the statistics looking for the WWIV event? Are we going to hit the attendance numbers we need?"

"I've been doing my best to get the word out, but it's tough to sell an exhibit about another war. We probably won't get our desired numbers, but it'll be close. It won't be a total flop."

The curator sighed. "I guess society just doesn't want to study history anymore. It's all about the newest or weirdest nowadays."

Kate's mind began to wander. She was looking forward to a lazy weekend, cooped up with her e-reader full of books, gaming, and gorging on forbidden chocolate. Forbidden because she knew she wouldn't spend the excess calories by working out. Her running clothes smelled moldy, as she hadn't bothered to wash them after last month's ten-minute attempt at a run. It was as good an excuse as any.

Before she settled down to relax, she went through a week's worth of email she'd been ignoring. Every night she had fallen into bed exhausted; now it was time to catch up with the bulging inbox. She grabbed her laptop and threw it on her disheveled bed. Then she stretched and got to work.

Waking at 10 AM the next morning, Kate felt her face being licked. It was Moongie, cleaning some melted chocolate off her forehead.

"Gross, Moongie!" She playfully shoved the cat away. She'd been lazy last night and had just started eating from a bag of chocolate chips. One must have fallen on her pillow before she fell asleep; she could see a smudge on it.

Not bothering to get out of bed, she rolled over, grabbing her smartphone to check for messages. Her laptop was out of reach; it had slipped off the bed during the night, landing on the cat's bed.

"I guess I have no choice, have to get out of bed. What do you think?" Moongie purred, then cleaned her fur. Finished being social for the day, the cat turned from her owner.

"I will be lazy today, just like you, Moongie. What do you think of that?"

Her cat continued to ignore her, so Kate got up with a groan and decided she'd better be at least a little productive. Maybe cleaning her apartment? She picked up a pile of dirty clothes tossed them in the closet and called it good. Kate's method of procrastination was hiding the mess and dealing with it later. Her laundry day coincided with running out of anything to wear.

Tomorrow the Pip5 was being released, and Kate couldn't wait to get one.

She knew firsthand just how great it was.

September 6, 2101

Kate looked warily at the overexcited guy speaking to her. She tried waiting for him to stop, but when he didn't, she cut him off.

"I'm trying to read my messages, so I can't really talk to you right now," said Kate.

"How long have you been waiting in line?" he asked.

"Me? I got here five minutes after you. So... about four hours."

Kate thought the guy was weird for asking her that question. He didn't wait for her answer; he'd already turned to the person in front of him to ask the same question.

She told herself for the hundredth time she'd never do this again, but she knew she would, and it bothered Kate. She couldn't believe she'd been sucked in once again by the hype. Her current phone worked well; it still looked new. She'd only owned it for a year, but she'd tested the new phone and knew it was superior to her current one. Plus, it was free. Her payment for taking part in the panel. She couldn't pass that up.

June 4, 2101

Kate locked up her bike in front of Pippin Corp headquarters. Curious about the consumer panel and not having anything else to do that night, she thought it would be an interesting way to spend a Saturday evening.

She walked into the gleaming monolith in awe of all the marble and glass *objet d'art* surrounding her. Kate spotted the information desk in the lobby and walked over to inquire about the location of the consumer panel.

The person manning the desk looked confused and asked for a few minutes to find out more. After several phone calls he turned and said, "Okay, I found the room number, just proceed up the elevator to the thirty-third floor. When you get there, the receptionist can direct you to the proper location. But first I need you to sign the guest book."

Kate signed in, thanked him, and took the elevator up, worried she was underdressed. Everyone looked so businesslike, and she was wearing jeans and her favorite gamer T-shirt. She smoothed down her shirt in a thwarted attempt to look professional.

The thirty participants seated in the room were

from the same demographic: early to midtwenties. An equal number of males and females sat around the table. Most racial and ethnic groups were represented. It was a mini cross-section of young Americans. Kate sat at the round table, waiting for the speaker to begin, happy to note no one else had dressed up.

"Welcome to Pippin Corp! We're quite pleased you accepted our invitation to join our panel. My name is Greg Zander and I'm the vice president of marketing. You all can call me Zander. If each of you would fill out your name badge and put it on, we can get started."

An assistant began passing them out and there was a small smattering of applause.

"Why don't we begin with everyone introducing themselves and telling us what you do for a living."

Groans from the group, eyes averted to avoid being first.

"I know, I know, it's an unpopular exercise. Tell you what, let's skip that step."

Louder applause. A couple of cheers.

"Our PR department has prepared a short film to introduce you to the product you'll be testing," said Zander. "Afterwards I'll go through the procedures and explain what we expect of you. Oh, and the best part, you will be rewarded for your time. More on that later."

For ten minutes, Kate and the rest of the group watched an overly caffeinated spokesman croon on video about the newest model of Pippin Corp's smartphone—the Pip5. It came in any color you wanted, as long as that color was red. That got a few laughs. It weighed a mere five ounces and had enough memory for thousands of songs, contacts, books, photos, and apps. The battery lasted for twelve hours and could be charged in thirty minutes when the battery was drained.

Kate's respiration increased, her eyes dilated, her heart raced. Her excitement over the Pip5 filled her body with endorphins. It was a feeling she experienced on two occasions—whenever she fell in love, which was rare, or went shopping. The lights came back on.

"I hope you enjoyed our little presentation," said Zander. "Before I can tell you anything else, you must sign the NDAs on the table in front of you."

Kate raised her hand. "What's an NDA?"

"Sorry for using acronyms, NDA stands for Non-Disclosure Agreement. We want none of you telling the competition about our fabulous new phone."

Forms signed and collected, Zander continued with his presentation.

"My assistant is passing around a bag for each of you. Inside, you'll find an instructional booklet, your test phone, and my business card. Please email me personally with any questions or comments."

Squeals and grunts of delight filled the room.

"Now, I'd mentioned being compensated for your time. How does a free Pip5 sound?"

Loud and prolonged applause.

"I knew you'd be excited. At the end of the study you'll each get a voucher for a free phone. Take it to your favorite electronics store and exchange the voucher for your new Pip5."

Kate thought of a question and raised her hand.

"Yes, you with the interesting T-shirt, I can't see your name badge," said Zander.

"Where are these smartphones produced?"

"Well, now, that's a conversation for another time, young lady. Okay, everyone, let's go through the instruction manual for the Pip5."

It seemed simple. All she had to do was promise to use the phone for two weeks and keep it near her during the entire duration of the test. Every two days she had to answer an online survey. At the end of two weeks she'd receive her voucher.

Kate left the conference room sure she'd made the right decision to help Pippin Corp. A free phone for so little effort! Saving money was a bonus since her salary at the museum wasn't enough to justify a new smartphone every year.

Yes, she thought, for once she'd made a decision she wouldn't regret.

A pimpled teen clerk dressed in the store's cobalt-blue uniform came out and addressed the large crowd using a megaphone. "Okay, people, the store will open in one hour. Please be patient. No shoving!"

The line snaked around the building and continued into the parking lot. The first dozen eager consumers had been sleeping in tents for days.

After checking her email for the twentieth time in an hour, Kate noticed another man. He was cycling past with a smile on his face. She noted his well-sculpted calves and knew he must do most, if not all, of his traveling on his bicycle. She smiled and averted her eyes, having caught his gaze. Kate appreciated his grin and admired his toned muscles before turning her attention back to her smartphone.

The huge double doors opened, allowing the crowd of shoppers into their version of nirvana. Thoughts of the cyclist were quickly replaced with a primal urge to consume. Kate shoved her old phone into her backpack with determination.

A large plasma screen looped an advertisement for the Pip5, emphasizing all the newest features.

"Never miss an appointment, wake up late, or miss your favorite show again. Activate the alarm and calendar features, and they will help you run your life. Turn off your brain and plug in to ours."

Kate watched the ad cycle through another fifty times before it was her turn to get her phone. None of the customers could pull their eyes away from the screen. At the end of each cycle she experienced the confusing desire to applaud.

Then, at last, it was in her hand. It was the thinnest one yet, barely five ounces and glossy red. Until you activated the touch screen, the front and back of the phone looked the same. Both sides were glossy, no differentiation between the two. She felt her usual buyer's rush, a gush of endorphins flooding her brain. It didn't matter that the phone was free. It was new. That fact was enough to feel the rush.

She boarded a bus to work, still giddy with greed, not realizing this would be her last day of happiness. It was that evening that most people in her region slept naturally for the last time.

Chapter 5

2102
One year AIB

There was still a small percentage of the population who were Sleepers. They kept their identities secret to survive. It was never proven that the missing Sleepers were dead, but none of the remaining people unaffected by sleeplessness wanted to take that chance. Their trust of President Glynis Grieves and her government waned once their friends went missing.

President Grieves. A president who never explained why no one could sleep or why this disaster happened. September 6, 2101 changed the United States. President Glynis Grieves, the leader of an insomnolent realm now known as the Nation. Encompassing the former states of Illinois and the southern part of Wisconsin, the Nation was split into four directional sectors, each with a city named after the sector's orientation. North City, South City, East City, and West City. The bureaucrats in charge of designing the area had little imagination.

When the insomnia pandemic began, the Sleepers reported to the CDC about their status and had the identity chips in their left wrists encoded with an S. After self-reporting, and without explanation, they disappeared, never to be seen or mentioned again. Government-run media never acknowledged the strange disappearances of the lucky ones.

The Sleepers were gone, and eventually the rest of the population forgot about them.

The remaining Sleepers chose silence, assumed new identities, and blended in with the rest of the populace or fled into the wilderness on the border of the Nation.

Claudia, a teacher in the time before, continued the education of the younger Sleepers in the compound. She'd left her husband, Samuel, behind in North City when she discovered he enjoyed the new sleepless existence. He claimed the extra hours gave him time to be more creative. She argued with him about the unnatural state of the world and how she detested the work they were now forced to do.

She worked in the food factory, controlling the machine that combined the ingredients into nutrition bars called EnUR-G. The only part she recognized were the dried herbs from the state-run farms. Bored after a few weeks, she requested a transfer to another task.

Claudia reported to the job assignment window in the Great Hall and asked for the current list of available tasks. Her eyes skimmed an unappealing assortment of ways to earn sleep.

The list was short.

Being an escort, which was just a nice way of saying prostitution.

Dismembering dead bodies. This included delivering them to a warehouse.

Euthanasia aide, i.e. giving a lethal dose of medicine to adult citizens unable to work.

Cleaning, which meant disposing of dead bodies from the Sector Games.

She had the sudden desire to share the list with Samuel so he could help her decide what to choose from this distasteful catalog, temporarily forgetting she couldn't. They'd been married three years now. A beautiful wedding two years before the pandemic—the last year had revealed Samuel's true nature. The memory came back to her before she could stop it.

"Claudia, I had the best day! When I went to the jobs window, Pete—you know Pete, the grumpy guy with the bad teeth—let me choose my task. That's never happened before. In the past it was always, 'Just do this one,' or 'A wimp like you? You're pretty useless, but how about this one?' Today—and I do not understand what changed—he said, 'What's your pleasure, mate?' Like he was English or something. Maybe he was distracted or whatever, but do you know what, Claudia? I asked to clean today."

"Wait, what? You *requested* a cleaning job?"

"Yeah, isn't that grand? I've always wanted to do something on my own and be near the forest. It was messy and I suppose gross, but I got to be alone and do this task with no one looking over my shoulder. I will ask to clean again. Plus, don't forget, I get one and a half times the credit! We can dream again. Green pill on weekends, maybe."

On that day, when he described cleaning for the first time and said it was exhilarating to be outside while working, she was stunned. Samuel's joy after performing such a disgusting task convinced Claudia it was time to leave. She loved him, but a voice in her head told her not to let him know she still slept.

"How was your day, Claudia? Did you find a new job?"

"I'm still trying to decide."

"Hey, honey, I love you, but these Somnum pills don't come cheap, and I can't keep earning for both of us. Aren't you out of pills yet?"

Claudia was a bad liar, so instead she changed the subject.

"So what will it be? Brown or black EnUR-G bar? I can mix up a salad to go with it."

Once Sam's red Somnum pill took effect, Claudia gathered her meager possessions and tiptoed out of their pod. She shook her head in amusement, realizing being quiet wasn't necessary. Sam wouldn't wake if she stomped out. The pills were strong, and once someone took one, they slept soundly the entire night. She snuck out in search of others of her kind. She hoped she wasn't the only Sleeper left. Her heart told her there were others. Taking a final look at the pod she'd shared with Samuel for the last year, Claudia was thankful they never had children.

Jeremy left his girlfriend once he realized he was one of the special few. He was tired of faking insomnia. After working in the Capitol and witnessing the inequality of life there versus in North City, he decided those people were no longer his society, his tribe. He moved to the city and took a job at the food factory.

Pre-pandemic Jeremy had made his living as a computer scientist specializing in hardware. He missed creating projects and resented wasting his talents at the food factory, but there were no technical jobs available. There were few people at the factory he found interesting except for one coworker, a former teacher.

During their lunch breaks Jeremy and Claudia talked about the good old days.

"Claudia, there's a seat at my table!" Jeremy made room by consolidating his stuff to his half of the table in anticipation of having a lunch companion.

Claudia smiled at her friend and walked toward

him. "Hey, Jeremy, another exciting day at the food factory, huh? So I was thinking about... before. You never told me what you did. I mean your previous profession. You know I used to teach, but after all these weeks of working together, you've never talked much about yourself."

"Sorry, it's...I just can't stand to remember how things were. I had a good life, and I miss it every. Single. Day. I'll tell you a little about it. But not today. I'm pretty sleepy. There was this poker game—"

Claudia looked at Jeremy with alarm on her face. "No! Please tell me you're joking. You could get into so much trouble..."

"Calm down, teacher," Jeremy said, patting her hand. "This was the first and only time I'll do something so stupid. Anyway, I played with some guys I've never met before and after a few hands, I'd lost all of my Somnum. Since we don't get paid for another day, I have to just power through and try to work today on no sleep." He shrugged. "Lesson learned."

Jeremy hated lying to Claudia about needing sleep, but caution was always a good idea. Something he noticed about her: He'd never seen her in line for Somnum. Daring to hope she was also a Sleeper, he worked up his courage to ask her. But the day he intended to ask, he found out she'd transferred to another task.

There were rumors of other Sleepers living on the outskirts of the city; he would find them and form his own tribe. A group that understood him and wouldn't sell him out to a government that ruled over the sleepless. Perhaps once he found them and got settled, he could go back for Claudia.

Decker never moved to the new city. When the pandemic was discovered and announced, he moved to the woods on the outskirts of the city, near the garbage wall. Others panicked, believing the rumors that the cities were the source of the problem, and they moved to the new area assigned to them. The new AIB government inferred that those who didn't move would die a painful, sleep-deprived death. Decker's new residence in North City was filled with paranoid, tired people. He wanted no part of it.

He was one of the last to leave his home. Decker resented being herded out of the city like cattle. Or sheep. Unlike the masses that tried to take everything they owned without success, Decker packed his red backpack. His drawing supplies, a journal, and photos of the paintings he left behind. Ever an optimist, he hoped this was a temporary situation and only packed enough clothes for two weeks.

Ten years later, he still wore the same clothes.

Chapter 6

2102
One year AIB

Decker tried to keep his memories from before the purge buried. Remembering the happy times made his current existence difficult. His ever-present smile was a facade meant to uplift the other Sleepers. But months after the beginning of insomnolence, he missed his old life. He wanted to be an artist again, to go for a run and admire the beautiful city he used to live in.

Tonight, he broke his rule. He thought about the first time he spotted Kate. It was one day before the plague of sleeplessness started.

September 6, 2101

Going for a run in his neighborhood, Decker felt annoyed at the people texting while walking. Their eyes glued to a glowing blue screen, not mindful of the world around them. He wished, as he did every time he saw those drones, they would look up once in a while.

Decker finished his run in the park, breathing heavily, sweat rolling into his blue eyes. His lips stretched into a smile when he saw the sunrise. Another gorgeous day, another chance to create a masterpiece. He walked the two blocks back to his loft apartment, cooling his muscles and giving him time to plan today's painting.

Passing a young woman transfixed by her screen, he greeted her with no hope of a response, "Gorgeous sunrise!" She met his expectation by not responding.

He watched her walk away and wondered when she'd last noticed anything worthwhile.

After his shower, Decker turned on the only non-essential electronic device he owned: his television. After he left his parent's home at eighteen, Decker pared his life down to what he considered important. His decision was not driven by economics but philosophy. Decker owned a stove, refrigerator, and an electric kettle.

He had no intention of going off-grid; he wanted to have what he needed based on the life he led. Growing up, he lived in a household full of gadgets. His parents were early adopters, gaining the first edition of everything. The newest television, the latest car, the fanciest phones.

Decker competed with objects for his parents' attention. Knowing they loved him made it worse. He viewed his parents as junkies. They couldn't help themselves.

"Hey, Mom, let's go to the zoo today, okay?"

Decker watched his mom playing a game on her phone, engrossed in matching pieces of fruit.

"Mom? It's sunny outside. I want to see the animals."

"Hmm? What? Oh sure, honey, give me a few more minutes."

Decker walked into his father's study.

"Hey, Dad, do you want to go to the zoo with Mom and me?"

His father was reading the owner's manual for his new car.

"Dad? Come on, I really want to go. You can drive your new car and check out the features on the way, okay?"

"What? Oh, great idea, son. My new baby needs to get broken in. Maybe we should go on a long drive today. What do you say?"

"I want to go to the zoo, Dad. It's one of my favorite places, plus I need to do a report on lions for school."

"But the zoo is only ten minutes away. Let's drive for two hours and see what my car can do."

He remembered how special he felt being in the car with his parents. This was a rare moment, when most of their attention was on him. The ten minutes flew by. His father talked about the new car's features while stroking the dashboard. His mother immersed herself in her game again.

They wound up at the zoo thirty minutes before closing, his father couldn't resist the temptation to go on a longer drive. Not asking the other passengers in the car if it was okay, he got on the highway and drove as fast as he could without getting a ticket. He stopped the car in front of the zoo's entrance and let his wife and son out.

Decker ran to the lion's cage so he could get information for his report. His mother took photos of the lions with her phone, then spent the rest of the time there tinkering with the picture, not interacting with her son. Decker could tell his mom's new photo filtering app had consumed her.

The drive home was silent, the air inside the car filled with disappointment.

The television was the only device he viewed as unnecessary, but he enjoyed watching it. He'd never owned a cell phone. Decker liked his time alone to create, think, read, and occasionally watch movies. Constant interruptions, and the expectation of immediate replies, didn't appeal to him.

Freedom in all forms. That's the way he lived.

Today's news made him laugh out loud. Another crowd waiting for the newest cell phone. He mentally corrected himself when he realized 'cell phone' was old school. Smartphone. He noted the group of campers at the front of the line and thought of the subject of his next painting. *Camping for Cell Phones.*

He liked the alliteration in the title, deciding against changing cell phone to smartphone. Before shutting off his television, he spotted the girl he'd greeted after his run. Not surprised she was in line, he studied her for a minute.

Pretty hot. Though Decker couldn't help but think she'd be more attractive if she weren't addicted to her phone.

He altered his plans. Decker rode his bike to the store and watched the people in line. Live sketches would be better for his new painting. If he ran into the girl, it would be a bonus. Changing into his cycling clothes, he arranged the subjects of his new painting in a scene in his head. Ready to go, he pedaled to the store.

Enjoying the cool fall weather, Decker wondered why he never felt the need to connect to anyone digitally. It wasn't only that he was put off by the idea due to his parents' obsession with those things; he never felt the *need* to own them.

He preferred face-to-face connections, touch. Decker would often reach out and touch a person's arm while speaking to them and almost never looked away from their face. Some looked uncomfortable when he did so, but for many it produced a smile on faces not used to such an intimate encounter.

Eye contact was important to Decker. He believed the

old adage about the eyes being the windows to the soul. He wasn't religious in the traditional sense, but felt that everyone had something inside that made him or her special. His paintings focused on the faces of his subjects, and Decker spent the most time on the eyes.

Decker didn't believe you could find that 'something' by speaking through a smartphone or on a video chat.

He placed his easel by the window to capture the natural light and sketched out his new piece. Drawing the big-box store proved to be the easiest element. They all looked alike. No beauty, just function.

Decker represented the line of customers waiting outside as sheep. Each woolly animal standing upright clutching their old smartphones. Their clothing and the expressions on their faces identified them.

Decker spent the most time sketching the girl he'd seen earlier. That ewe had long, curly red wool for hair, a black miniskirt, and a purple backpack. Her expression proved the most difficult for him to draw. But after erasing several times, he nailed it.

She looked lost.

The sketch was complete, now for the paint selection. Watercolor wasn't bold enough, so Decker went with acrylics. One problem: He didn't have enough colors. Time to hop on his bicycle again.

The art store was near the big-box store, which pleased him. Decker would have an excuse to go in and observe the sheep once more. He needed to make a few more notes for his masterpiece.

Locking his bike outside the store, he walked in hoping to see the redhead again. Greeting Decker at the front door was a cheerful employee with a false smile. He offered Decker a card with a number on it.

Decker was confused. "What's this for?"

Now the greeter looked confused. "Hey, man, aren't you here for the new Pip5 phone?"

"Uh, no, thanks, just want to browse for awhile."

The greeter shook his head. Decker decided the kid thought he was either crazy or a shoplifter. Either way, Decker heard him radio security to keep an eye on 'the guy in the spandex shorts.'

Every aisle of the store seemed to be deserted except for the area near the service desk. The line snaked back and forth, Disneyland style. Scanning the crowd, he spotted her, the redhead.

Be cool, Decker told himself. *Don't act like a stalker. Don't be weird. Stay away and take notes on the rest of the sheep.*

Decker found a viewpoint in the video-game aisle. From there he could observe the crowd while pretending to check out the latest games. He opened his sketchpad and worked on his drawings.

After a few minutes, he stopped; he could feel the eyes of the redheaded girl staring at him.

Chapter 7

February 9, 2111

Today was Kate's birthday. No one celebrated holidays or marked anniversaries of any kind now. Celebrations weren't illegal, but there didn't seem to be any point. Kate's rebellious side sang the traditional *Happy Birthday* song to herself every year. If she was alone, she sang the song aloud. Kate felt ancient today, but in truth she'd just turned thirty-three. The last time she celebrated her birthday with another person was ten years ago. As she did every year on her birthday, she wished Grandmother Bridget could be with her to celebrate.

Ten long, sleepless years.

Guess I'm stuck doing this cleanup by myself. I CAN DO THIS! I CAN DO THIS! I can do this? I NEED to do this!

Walking to the subway station, trying not to think about where she was headed, Kate thought about the first time she couldn't sleep. That evening, she didn't understand her first night of insomnia would soon become the norm for her and thousands of others.

September 6, 2101

She'd experienced sleepless nights before; during college it happened at least twice a month. The stress of classes or trying to pull an all-nighter to study for an exam was an accustomed part of her life. It used to be a point of pride to say you'd stayed up all night.

The first night she couldn't sleep didn't alarm Kate. It was the third night that frightened her. By the fourth night she panicked. The next morning she and the rest of the newly sleepless received a plain red box. The return address said *Centers for Disease Control*.

Inside the box, a small bottle labeled *Somnum* contained seven red pills. The instructions said to take one pill per night to sleep. The accompanying brochure explained that once the pills ran out, she would have to earn more. Any explanation of the mass insomnia was missing.

It was the start of an unending nightmare.

February 9, 2111

Kate jumped on the ITS, swiping the chip in her left wrist to pay her fare. She missed cash; it was too easy to spend money without a physical form. She never had credit cards before; cash only for her.

Not that there was anything to spend her hard-earned credit on other than sleep. Nice clothes? No. Vacations? Hah. There was no such a thing. She could pay extra credits for the green Somnum dream pills, but why? Dreams would only make her miss her old life and give her hope. Hope, nothing but a dangerous false emotion.

Her meager credits—meager in her opinion, compared to how she earned them—were for sleep and only sleep. The government, in exchange for total allegiance to the President and her policies, provided food and shelter to its citizens. *More like an emperor or dictator,* Kate thought.

Her spare credits paid for her limited wardrobe. Limited due to the lack of selection. To simplify her life, she purchased the same outfit over and over. Dark-green pants, combat boots, a tan khaki jacket, and a red shirt. Function over form. She used to care how she looked and on days she allowed herself to reminisce, thought wistfully about her closet full of clothes.

Finding an empty car on the train, Kate sat facing a poster.

NEED BONUS SLEEP? CALL 767VJM.

Those posters intrigued her; the thought of bonus sleep was difficult to pass up. But she'd asked around and been told the cost was too high. No one was specific about the payment but inferred she would not want to pay.

Nothing for nothing. Or was it something for nothing?

God, I need to sleep, I can't even be sarcastic.

She felt her real self fading away bit by bit.

Her destination was still three stops away, so she slipped her messenger bag over her head and slung it across her shoulders. It was filled with the tools she needed for the cleanup. Kate hoped there would be an energy station at her stop; her lack of sleep was affecting her coordination. She needed the temporary jolt to get through her task.

Not for the first time, she wondered why she was cursed with permanent insomnia. Kate wondered if the President and her cabinet suffered the same malady she did.

For a few seconds she reminisced about coffee, and her job as a barista. She'd hated that job, but the perk of unlimited cups of java was something she missed. Kate wished she'd appreciated that aspect of her employment at *The Cup*. The smell used to make her salivate like Pavlov's dog. Her then boyfriend would deliver a cup to her bedside every morning. All she had to do was roll over, breathe in the addictive aroma, and feel her mouth water. She missed those mornings, but not the boyfriend. He turned out to be a terror.

They'd met when both of them took part in a consumer-testing panel at Pippin Corp, before the nightmare of insomnolence. She, along with thirty others, had been chosen to test the newest smartphone about to be released. A free phone and a boyfriend. At the time she thought she'd won the lottery. After that disastrous relationship, she shied away from any close connections.

One day she would explain that to Decker, but she wasn't ready. Maybe then she could tell him she'd noticed him ten years ago.

"Hey, Kate! Wait up!" Kate heard someone running toward her.

Stepping away from the subway turnstile, she spotted Decker. She stopped and smiled, waving to her friend with a mixture of excitement and surprise. "How did you find me? I need your company on a cleanup. You in?"

He jogged toward her, grinning. "How can I say no to you? Lead the way. I'm all yours till the job is done."

They took the antiquated escalator to the surface, passing peeling posters with advertisements for things that no longer existed, catching up since the last time they'd met. Decker never kept the same schedule to prevent discovery, so Kate only saw him when he sought her out. He'd never told her where he lived and she resisted asking him. She knew as a Sleeper he was in danger, and if she knew his location they'd both be in peril. Neither of them wanted that. But it didn't stop Kate from wondering how he spent his time when he wasn't with her.

Glancing up at his profile, she noticed new lines around his eyes. He was too young for those, and she assumed the premature network of lines was a result of his fugitive lifestyle, the stress of being a Sleeper showing on his face.

"So who's on the menu today, Kate?" He smirked at her. "Did you actually read their dossier this time?"

Kate paused and stared at him. Decker shifted his eyes away, and she wondered if he was hiding something from her. Kate stepped off the escalator and kept walking, trying to speed up. She couldn't look backward at Decker; her face would give away too much.

"Hey, I was kidding. Come on, Kate, if we don't make this fun why should I play?"

Kate stopped, bringing her hands up to her face. She covered her eyes and dug the heels of her hands into her eyeballs. Her body trembled as she slumped down to the filthy floor of the ITS station.

"I'm so tired, Decker, so tired..."

They'd established the parameters of their friendship; hugging was not part of it. Kate wanted Decker to reach for her, but she was adamant about no physical affection, and he seemed to accept this condition so he could be around her.

"Hey, there's a ViGor station over there in the corner, want me to get you a shot? I scored extra units, I can buy it for you."

His hopeful eyes scanned Kate's exhausted face. She knew he was lying about the credits but didn't question him about it.

"That'd be great, Decker, thanks."

Decker walked over to the bright neon machine. From where she sat, Kate could see photos of energetic workers adorning the dispenser of false energy. She knew there would be a small, seldom-noticed sign at the bottom that said, "A Pippin Corp Product." Kate wondered why Pippin Corp made ViGor. They were an electronics company specializing in smartphones. Not having the energy to think anymore about it, she pushed the thought away and waited for Decker to return.

Decker purchased two auto-injectors, the second one for insurance in case the cleanup took longer than anticipated. Kate needed the extra energy to get back to the Great Hall and cash in her completed work order.

Clutching the auto-injector with shaking hands, Kate dosed herself in her thigh. The artificial energy coursed through her body, gifting her with the illusion of wakefulness. She had two hours before exhaustion took over again. She silently thanked the inventor of ViGor while cursing the woman who made coffee illegal. Kate wondered why everyone else had to suffer because President Grieves didn't like coffee. Another example of how the President was selfish and out of touch with the people.

Opening what passed for food now, Kate ate the black EnUR-G bar, washing it down with water. Pulling out a bag of strawberries, grown on one of the Nation's farms, she offered them to Decker. He refused. Refreshed for the moment, she rose and walked toward the exit. Confident Decker would follow, she wasted none of her precious energy to tell him she was ready to work. Her focus was on arriving at the cleanup and starting the dreaded task.

She couldn't afford the emotional or physical energy to think about anything else.

Chapter 8

February 9, 2111

Decker and Kate walked in silence for several minutes before they reached their destination. Kate, trying to reserve energy, set a slow pace. She kept her focus on the ground, convincing her tired body she could walk one more step. She imagined washing herself off after the cleanup and lying down for a blissful evening of sleep. As they approached the arena, she stopped and at last spoke to Decker.

"I haven't had to do a cleanup in a while," she said. "I know I said never again, but this is an emergency. The damned server glitched, and I thought I had more sleep credits left."

Decker looked at her sympathetically.

"I need to learn to sew. Then maybe I can work in the clothing factory. Anything, well, almost anything, would be better than this."

"What if you mov—"

"I've told you I don't want to move to the Capitol," she said, sighing. "But if the only job I get here is cleaning up, I may change my mind."

Decker nodded. "No, you're right, not the Capitol. You would be miserable there. Hey, I'll take care of it today. Just keep me company, okay?"

Kate wanted to feel grateful, but irritation took over. "You know I can't just keep you company! The only way I get credit is to perform the cleanup myself! Or did you forget about the flash drive in my head? This is serious, Decker. You're not helping."

The flash drive recorded her doing the job. Once she accessed the start code, she was stuck. Her rage exhausted her; she trembled again.

"Hey, cool down. I have a surprise for you. We... um... I have been working on a special little project."

He reached into his backpack, rummaging around until he found a small black flash drive. It looked identical to the one in Kate's head.

"This beauty will become whoever I program in. So... I can put it in the Imitator, set it for Kate, and the data gets recorded as if you did the job."

Eyes widening with understanding, Kate almost smiled. Instead she said, "Who's we? And what's an Imitator? Are you hiding something from me?"

"A mere slip of the tongue, Katie girl." He ducked as she swung at him playfully; he knew she disliked her old name. She'd used the more adult form of her name after she was hired for what she considered a real job, instead of her nickname, Katie. It made her feel more professional.

"Seriously, though, I worked on this project and programmed you into it so you'll never have to do a cleanup again. Now where are my thanks?"

He leaned in dramatically for a kiss. After a few seconds he straightened up, pretending to be offended at being ignored. He pulled out a little silver box the size of a deck of cards from a front pocket of his backpack.

"Meet the Imitator. This bit of a machine loads the details of the job onto your drive and *voilà*, you get credit!" Decker bowed to Kate.

Kate watched Decker insert a flash drive into the machine while explaining the rest of the process. "Once I finish the cleanup job, I add your flash drive along with the one already in this device."

Kate lunged at Decker and gave him a hug, and she could tell he was shocked. After a few seconds, he ended the embrace so he could continue the demonstration.

"Wait, you don't have a port," she said. "How will this work?"

Decker dug into his backpack for one more item. He pulled out a hat with a strap, which apparently was to hold the Imitator in place.

"Look inside. See the silver dots? They read what my eyes see by accessing my brain and relay the information to the flash drive. Pretty cool, don't you think?"

Kate was quite impressed. She didn't know Decker had the skills to build anything like this.

"Where did you get the materials to make that?" she asked. "It's not like there are stores where you can buy the stuff."

"There's a place with loads of free stuff—it's called the Garbage Wall," he said with mock amazement. "You'd be surprised at what's there. It took time, but after a few weeks of scavenging, I found everything I needed. The only things not available in the Wall are clothes. All of it rotted after ten years of rain, sun, and snow. I'm tiring of wearing the same things, but I digress."

Kate laughed. She loved Decker's way of thinking. She wouldn't have considered the Wall as a shopping center.

"So what else did you find there?"

"Why, you want to go shopping?"

"Not that it's important, but if you ever see an mp3 player, would you grab it for me? Mine is old and I'm getting tired of my playlist."

"Anything for you, Katie. I'll keep an eye out."

She gave him the evil eye for calling her Katie again.

"To make things more realistic, remind me to put some of the gunk on your boots. Blood and guts should do the trick. Maybe a spatter on your arms as well?"

Turning her around, he parted her hair, reaching for the flash drive. She blushed as his fingers brushed the back of her neck. She could feel Decker's breath on her skin, and it caused her entire body to shiver.

"Stop wiggling, I need to remove your drive."

As Decker pulled the drive out, Kate thought about their relationship. On the surface, they acted as if they were brother and sister. She'd set limits early on, not because she wasn't attracted to Decker, she just didn't think she'd ever be ready for the complication of being in love. Not in this version of her reality. A joyful relationship didn't seem possible since she spent most of her time performing tasks to earn sleep.

There were days she regretted her harsh rule, though. Whenever Decker was in her personal space—which for Kate was about a foot away—she felt his energy and trembled. This usually caused her to back up into safe territory, but for some reason, today she needed to stand close to him.

They entered the arena, a forested area with high stone columns and barbed-wire fencing. Strewn around the arena were bloody discarded weapons. Kate could see swords, a dented shield, and a spear. In the center lay two corpses—the losers of the latest tournament. From a distance they appeared to be asleep, but Kate knew the truth. She didn't bother to keep track of which Sector team was in the lead. She didn't care. Before insomnolence began, she never followed sporting events. Now she had less reason to root for a particular team. Being aligned with a team or player meant condoning the death of players from the other teams. It all seemed barbaric to her.

Kate shook her head in grim amusement,

remembering her thoughts on American football. The sport she'd once thought too violent would have been preferable to this. Any other game would be better. Competition involving deaths hadn't occurred since Ancient Rome, when the gladiators fought. She wondered if the President was a fan of ancient history, or more to the point, thought herself an empress with the power of life or death at her disposal. No, Kate thought, President Grieves was a sadist. There could be no other explanation for her creation and support of the Series.

Kate knew Decker was a sports fan, enjoying individual sports like track, skiing, and tennis. He'd told her once these tournaments were not sport—they were a sign of the devolution of their society. He was sickened by the carnage.

"Not as messy as usual. How kind of them to die neatly in a pile."

Kate stared at him, shocked.

"Geez, Kate, don't you know when I'm joking?" Stepping toward her, he reached for her hand. "Come on, it's me!"

"I know, but it scares me to hear you joke like that. If you keep making jokes about horrible things, you'll lose your humanity. Who would I turn to then?" She looked away. "How did we get here, Decker? Why is it acceptable to watch people die in the name of sport? Am I too sensitive? Or has the world just become coarser?"

She allowed Decker to continue holding her hand,

enjoying the calming effect of his touch. Kate's shivering ceased.

"Let me get started while you rest, Kate. There's a spot under that tree that looks comfortable. Go there and wait for me. Don't turn around. That way you won't see what needs to be done."

"But—"

"I know you've seen it before, but I don't want you to see anything like this again. I'm serious, Kate. No joking. I'm here so you don't have to be a part of this." He gestured toward the duo of bodies.

Kate moved her exhausted body to the tree, dropped to her knees, and leaned against the trunk. Staring into the forest, she pretended the world hadn't changed. She daydreamed about the nights she'd slept in her comfortable four-poster bed, cuddling with Moongie. She missed Moongie terribly. The CDC wouldn't let Kate take her cat with her when she was evacuated from her apartment. Moongie and Kate both cried as she left. Moongie's heartbreaking yowl the last thing she heard before being led away.

Trying to drown out the sound of Decker working, she jammed earplugs in, listening to her favorite music, thankful she'd remembered to grab her mp3 player when she had to leave her apartment a decade ago. She hoped Decker would be able to find her a replacement when it wore out. At the Garbage Wall Shopping Center. She smiled at her little joke as she stared at the sky, trying not to think about what Decker was doing.

Chapter 9

February 8, 2111

Pete sat behind the counter watching the line of eager citizens. Everyone looked haggard, but that was to be expected. This was the line for the Somnum pills. The valuable pills that endowed the recipient with the gift of slumber. He had the power of sleep at his disposal and reveled in it.

Pete remembered a time when sex and food were at the top of his list. He hadn't had sex in years, not by choice. Food all tasted the same now, so that wasn't anything to relish. The only thing he looked forward to was his evening appointment with his pillow. Sleep, the dream-free version, was all he desired. His reward for getting through another boring day in insomnia city.

He couldn't understand the ones that spent their hard-earned credits on the green pill. Dreams made you hope. Hope was dead, so why fool yourself? When he was more bored than usual, Pete liked to guess which of the people in line would request the green

Somnum pill. Most wanted the standard red; it cost fewer credits and didn't burden them with useless dreams.

Eyeing the people in line, he didn't see his favorite. Pete never bothered to use her actual name; he preferred to call her Curly. He liked her short, curly auburn hair and her attitude. She'd be fun. The old kind of fun he never seemed to want to have anymore. He tried to remember the last time he'd had sex and couldn't.

Damn shame.

Pete's attention returned to the woman in front of him. She seemed nervous, trying to get his attention by making direct eye contact. Conversations consisting of words other than 'red' or 'green' were rare, so when this next customer greeted him, Pete became suspicious. "Hello there, how's your day going?"

Pete replied with his standard grunts, but the customer persisted. "I heard you might have a, uh... special going on. Remus told me."

"I don't know anyone named Remus," he snapped. "Green or red?"

The disappointed woman walked away clutching her red pills. Pete hoped she'd ask him the same question later tonight. Maybe he could collect something more exciting than potatoes and fruit. Then he laughed; he knew he couldn't go through with anything physical. His wife was dead, but it would feel like cheating to him. But he could pretend.

Three weeks ago he fired Remus. They'd been in business together for six months. Six wonderful, profitable months. Then Remus got greedy. He didn't think Pete was charging enough for the pills. So whenever Remus sold the product, his euphemism for the pills, he added to the price.

January 18, 2111

The two of them had agreed to meet in the break room of the Great Hall, and Remus was going to convince that jerk that he deserved a bigger cut. He entered the room carrying a backpack bulging with contraband. He gave Pete a smile and grabbed a chair, scooting it across the floor to join him.

"Hey, Pete. How's it going, buddy? I got some product for us to move."

"Yeah? So how much did you pay this time? Did they raise the price? Give me some good news here."

"Nah, don't worry. This was a clean transaction. We get the Somnum and all they want is some more of your excellent liquor. Same amount as last time. One bottle for one hundred pills."

"So no one at the pill factory suspects anything? You still dealing with the same person?" asked Pete.

"I told you, I've got it handled. Now come on, we gotta count out these pills and bag 'em for our clients. We're going to corner the market on these. Since no one else is selling them I guess we have a monopoly, yeah?"

"I heard a rumor about you, Remus."

"Yeah, what about?"

Remus looked defensive, and that confirmed what Pete suspected.

"You've been charging more for the Somnum than I do," said Pete. "I heard you're making the buyers do things for you. Things I'm not comfortable with. I've been thinking about it, and we need to go our separate ways. I'll give you some extra pills to sell, but don't come back for any more. I'm going to our contact at the pill factory tomorrow to let them know about this."

"What the hell, man, you can't do this! We're partners!"

"Don't make a scene, Remus. Get out."

Remus stood up angrily, muttering what Pete believed to be threats. But as expected, the gutless dirtbag did nothing and left.

Pete charged one pound of fruit or vegetables for every five pills. The rumors he'd heard said Remus charged a sexual favor in addition to the regular price. It was probably still a bargain in Remus' opinion, but the idea repulsed Pete. They made liquor from the food they collected; asking for sex from the female customers was crossing a line.

After thinking about it, Pete realized he really didn't need Remus, but Remus definitely needed him.

Green pill tonight when I go to bed, he thought. *I need to remember what it's like to hold a woman in my arms.*

He hoped he dreamed about Jean.

After work, the first thing Pete did when he entered his pod was check his messages. Business had been picking up lately, ever since he'd had signs placed on the subway. The police hadn't forced him to take down his advertisements, which meant the bribes he paid were enough to satisfy the leeches. Good thing he had enough of his homemade booze to pay off everyone.

President Grieves would never see the signs; she didn't take the ITS. The blinking amber light on his box meant customers. Lots of desperate customers—his favorite type. Pete would check the messages later after he relaxed for an hour or so. Being an asshole all day was exhausting.

The second part of his homecoming routine was to check his stash of extra pills. No one knew where he hid them, but lots of people knew he had them. Pete was paranoid someone would come into his pod while he was working and rip him off. Especially Remus. Satisfied all was well in his tiny home, he opened a cabinet and chose his dinner.

Black bar or brown bar?

For some variety, he chose the brown bar. He shook his head when he noticed the bars displayed a new label: Brown EnUR-G. No name change would improve the taste of them, but you would think the manufacturer would at least try. He'd tried tan bars and the black ones. Although marketed as different flavors, to his unsophisticated palate, there was no difference. Never one for fruits or vegetables, this was the only other food available in North City. He salivated remembering the last time he ate a steak. The thought angered him. He'd been turned into a vegetarian against his will.

As he opened the brown bar, he pretended it was a filet mignon cooked rare, with a huge pile of fluffy mashed potatoes. Brown gravy dripping down the mountain of white. Next to his perfect meal, a glass of Cabernet Sauvignon. This pretense was the only way he could choke down the disgusting version of meals he and everyone else was forced to consume. Pete suspected the president and her cronies didn't eat this slop. Liquor helped him wash down the tasteless EnUR-G bar.

Switching on the television, Pete had a choice of three stations.

Channel 1: News

Channel 2: Sports

Channel 3: Government

A bit of sport sounded appealing, so he turned to Channel 2. Maybe he was in time to watch the fights. He hoped so. The Sector Series had begun this morning while he was at work, but the matches often lasted the entire day. If the match proved to be epic, it went on until the next morning.

The twenty-inch screen of his ancient television filled with a forest. He'd been issued a standard vidscreen just like the one everyone else had. It sat unopened in the corner. He preferred his old television; it reminded him of his previous life.

As the camera panned out, Pete could see one of his favorite features of the arena, the forty-foot-tall barbed-wire fence. He wondered if anyone else appreciated the beauty of barbed wire. He knew each ranch in the old Western States had a unique style of wire.

When he'd worked on a ranch before moving to Chicago, he'd enjoyed repairing the fences because it was one of the rare times he could be alone and not answer to the owner. He missed the fresh air and a job that worked up a sweat. Sitting all day in the Great Hall was making him soft. No, not just soft. Lazy and soft. His flabby belly was proof of that.

The camera zoomed in on the two teams, West and East. Pete was disappointed; he was a fan of North, his home sector, but this would do. North would play after this first match. Pete needed to relax after a long day, so any match was fine as long as it took his mind off his work.

The fighter from the winning team would be exhausted yet would be expected to fight the North player without a break. The teams were still choosing their weapons, so he had missed little. Pete made himself comfortable, ready to watch the carnage.

Chapter 10

February 8, 2111

Remus wasn't in a good mood. He resented Pete's corner on the sleeping pill black market and wanted in on the action. They'd begun as partners in the pill business, but three weeks ago, after a trifling incident—at least according to Remus—Pete kicked him out.

Revenge. Remus wanted it, and at last he'd figured out how to get it. He'd go to the police station and report Pete. There was the risk of getting arrested himself, but at this point Remus' anger trumped common sense.

He stood in front of the station practicing his speech. Instead of confessing to being part of Pete's scheme, Remus would say he did it to catch a black-market scumbag for the police. He hoped his fake altruism would fool them.

Remus entered the building and looked for someone official.

"Uh, excuse me. I need to speak with someone to report a crime."

A bored-looking sergeant looked up from his messy desk, answering Remus.

"You can tell me. What is it? Come on, buddy, I'm busy here."

Remus had heard on the news that the police had lots of cases and figured this officer didn't want to add to his workload. Remus paused, not sure how to proceed. This sergeant might not be the right person to talk to. He looked around the room and spotted a younger officer.

"Never mind, I see you're busy, sir. I'll talk to the guy over there. Sorry to bother you."

"Fine," he said, waving him off, "just move along and stop annoying me."

Remus approached the other officer and asked where he should go to report a crime, and this time he got the reaction he wanted.

"A crime? You're in the right place. What are you reporting?" This officer seemed happy to help.

After reporting on Pete's black-market pill operation and convincing the police officer he was an innocent party, he waited. Remus sat in a rusted chair, figuring it was a good sign he hadn't been arrested. This was going easier than he'd expected.

"Sir, I need you to follow me to a different office," said the officer.

"Sure, sure. Whatever you need from me. Just trying to be a good citizen."

The officer led Remus to the Capitol building, and on to the office of one of the President's aides. As soon as it became apparent where they were headed, Remus began to sweat profusely.

"Good luck, sir," the officer said before leaving him.

Being addressed as 'sir' startled him. It was the first time anyone had called him that. His nerves began to get the better of him, not knowing if this was a good or bad thing was making him twitch. Was he about to be arrested after all? After a few minutes an official-looking man walked in and greeted Remus.

"Hello, my name is Andrew. I'm President Grieves' senior aide. I hear you have some news you'd like to pass on to her."

"Well, yes, I do. I was telling the officer about this guy who is selling black-market Somnum. Being the good citizen that I am—"

"Enough bullshit. What are you offering?"

"No bullshit, sir, I want to let you know about the scoundrel, Pete Sanderson."

"And what do you get out of this?"

"Just doing the right thing, sir. But... I wouldn't mind a little reward."

"Of course you wouldn't." He frowned at Remus. "Why do you consider this information important? Do you think it matters to us if someone is selling some pills?"

Remus considered this and changed his tactic.

"The other thing I wanted to tell you is I suspect this guy Pete is actually an agent for the Sleepers." Remus hoped Andrew couldn't tell he was lying.

"Now that is interesting information. Stay here for a few minutes while I speak with President Grieves."

Andrew left the room. Remus fidgeted, wondering if he'd gone too far. He scoped out the exits in case he needed to make a quick escape. Andrew returned ten minutes later.

"Well, Remus, the President is indeed interested in your information. She's instructed me to tell you to spy on Pete with the end goal of trying to infiltrate the Sleepers. She wants you to find their location and to figure out if they are up to anything."

"What does th—"

"By up to anything, I mean, are they planning to rise up against the government? Are they trying to leave? Information like that will be worth a large reward."

Remus swallowed with anticipation. "How large?"

Andrew smirked. "Let's just say you'll have enough credits to never have to do a job again to get Somnum. Now go away, and don't come back until you have something to report."

Remus didn't have to be told twice. He was excited at this new development. Now he had an official mission: to infiltrate the Sleepers.

After leaving the police station, Remus contemplated how to go about completing his new task. He figured the best way to spy on Pete was to follow him around, so all day he sat on the far end of the Great Hall to observe Pete distributing pills to the sleeping masses. At the end of the day, Remus followed him to his pod. He couldn't believe what a boring life Pete led. Remus wondered how long he could continue to follow him.

Two days after he began his surveillance, Remus received an odd call. Someone called asking to purchase some Somnum. But that wasn't the odd part. The caller told him he got the number from a sign on the ITS.

This could be promising. Wonder what the kid is really after?

That night, after failing to show up for their appointment, a kid appeared at Pete's pod window. He climbed in carrying a backpack. Remus assumed it was the caller.

Should I stop this kid or wait to see what he's up to?

Remus watched as the stranger ransacked the pod, looking for something. Remus knew it had to be the sleeping pills. There was nothing else valuable inside, and it turned out he was right. The kid jumped out of the window and ran toward the ITS. Remus followed him, getting on the car next to the thief. He had a good feeling about this. When the train arrived at the final stop, all the remaining passengers departed.

Remus wondered where the kid was going; there

wasn't much near the last stop. He watched as the thief broke into a run, heading north. Remus groaned. He wasn't much of an athlete, but lucky for him, he spotted an abandoned bicycle just outside the ITS station. He hopped on and followed from a safe distance so the thief wouldn't notice him.

Two miles later, it was getting more and more difficult to stay hidden, so Remus had to abandon the bike and hide in the forest, which was getting denser the farther away from the city they traveled. Remus looked around, surprised to see such a lush forest. He and everyone else in the city believed there was nothing but a wasteland outside the border of the city, and now that he was here, he wasn't sure why he'd never thought to come see for himself. Or why no one else did, either. After all, nothing had stopped him.

After what seemed like forever, the kid took a sharp left and disappeared.

"Damn it!" Remus cursed. Where did he go?

Chapter 11

T he team from the East Sector ate dinner at a communal table in their dormitory. The long tabletop was filled with delicacies Ling hadn't seen since BIB. Bowls piled high with rice, grilled vegetables, and something she thought no longer existed: red meat. She wondered where it came from. It also made her suspicious of the things she'd been told over the years by the government. They claimed the Nation was the only surviving part of the United States. If this was true, where did they get this food? There were no domesticated animals to provide the meat, and the farms didn't grow rice. Ling tried to be grateful for the feast, but it still bothered her. She wanted her parents to partake of this. For that matter, she wanted all the citizens of the Nation to take advantage of this bounty. Ling found she couldn't enjoy her meal, not properly. Every bite tasted like betrayal.

She looked around at her other teammates—they didn't look surprised. They were all greedily gobbling down the food. Their coach walked around the table, encouraging them all to eat as much as they could, explaining that the protein from the meat would strengthen them and help them in their fights. When the coach got to Ling, he stopped and asked her, "Everything okay here? You don't appear to be eating as much as your teammates. You need to take advantage of this, Ling. I've watched you in training and am concerned that you may have some problems when you fight tomorrow. I almost traded you out for another player, then changed my mind. You have to fight sometime, so tomorrow is your big day. Eat up! Perhaps this meal will give you the edge you need."

Ling changed her mind about being in the Sector Series after the meal. Something wasn't right about the whole competition. If they were being lied to about the food that was available, what else was false?

Her noble plan to win seemed crazy now. She'd never handled a weapon until her training with the East Sector team. No matter how much she practiced, she achieved no level of competence. Her coach forced her to spend hours watching previous fights so she could learn how to compete. When the team found out which player would fight this time, Ling watched him in the hopes of discovering any weaknesses in his style. She couldn't find any. He—she didn't want to learn his name ahead of time—seemed assertive and strong. Every video she watched sapped her confidence.

That evening, she ran away after trying to talk to one of her teammates about her doubts. She was met with a dull stare as if what she was saying made no sense to him. Fearing she'd said too much, Ling knew she had to leave right away. Worried he'd report her to the coach, she snuck out of the dormitory her team slept in, carrying a small bag of her belongings.

Without a plan, she headed toward the East Sector, hoping someone there would hide her. She couldn't ask that of her parents. They wouldn't be able to offer any help, and Ling was already worried about the dishonor her desertion would bring them. She knew they'd understand and be happy she chose life, but in their culture, the dishonor of backing out would be a terrible shame for them to bear.

It was 2 AM when she found a place to take a short rest. Ling enjoyed climbing trees, and this one had a comfortable spot for her to rest and gave her a clear view of the area. The moon was out, allowing her to see any person approaching her. In her haste, she'd forgotten to bring her Somnum pills, so sleep wasn't an option. Sitting for a bit and trying to organize her thoughts seemed to be the best idea. What the future held was hard for her to picture. Running forever wasn't viable, but Ling couldn't allow herself to think she'd made a mistake. If she thought that, she'd turn herself in now.

The day Ling applied for the Sector Series had been a proud moment for her. Being selfless, giving all to her family—that was how her parents raised her. Filial devotion was a part of her parents' heritage. If her mother and father knew she was running away, they would feel the shame of her betrayal for the rest of their lives. Ling worried it might even be enough to kill her father. But she also hoped that the knowledge she was still alive somewhere would bring them some measure of joy.

Hours later, ready to move on after her rest, Ling heard the voices of the police searching for her. She ducked down and waited for them to pass. She overheard snippets of their conversation as they walked beneath her hiding place.

"Pain-in-the-ass girl..."

"Thoughtless..."

"Hope she gets a sword in the gut after all the trouble she's causing us."

The voices died down. Ling leapt from the tree limb, landing on a mound of moss. Blood pounding in her ears, she held her breath, trying to calm herself so she could listen for the police. Thinking she'd avoided capture, Ling headed away from the police and ran. More voices. One of the officers spotted Ling and yelled to the others. She ran but was overtaken after a few minutes. One of the officers threw her to the ground.

Capture.

"Please don't make me go back," she cried. "I can't do this. I'm the only one who takes care of my parents. What if I die? What then?"

"Should have thought about that before you volunteered, girl," said an older officer.

The group of officers waited for her to comply.

"Can't you just ignore me and pretend you never found me? Please, I'm begging you!"

"I'll pretend you didn't say that to me. Now stand up and come with us. There's no turning back now. You have to compete today. No backing out. You knew the rules when you volunteered. What's wrong with you, girl? It's an honor to represent your sector in the games."

The older officer prodded her with his stick.

Ling thought of her parents once more, remembered her reason for competing. How could she have been so stupid? Her goal was to help her parents and honor them, not bring them shame. Ling lowered her head, feeling the heat on her face as she realized what an utter failure she was. She couldn't outrun the entire force and had no place to go. Her dream of freedom had been foolish.

She straightened her back and marched toward her fate.

Chapter 12

February 8, 2111

The announcer said there'd been a delay due to a missing player from the East. She'd been found minutes ago, claiming she didn't realize today was the start of the Sector Series. An investigation would follow and appropriate punishment would be meted out to her coach after the games were finished.

The referee counted to three, then the captain of the team with the best record at that point chose heads or tails. The time honored coin-toss ritual of deciding which team chose first.

"Well, it looks like West will start by choosing their weapons first," said the announcer.

Pete liked the ancient weapons; he was never a fan of guns or lasers. Crossbows, spears, maces, swords—they seemed more honorable. He used to read books about knights in the Middle Ages. The thought of fighting with honor had always appealed to him. Being forced to fight close enough to see the eyes of your enemy was a better way to go.

Although he didn't routinely agree with the government's decisions, he thought the rule to conduct the fight using these types of weapons was one of the best things they'd ever decreed. He had to admit he took a certain amount of satisfaction in the decision to have teenagers do the fighting, though he told himself it wasn't out of cowardice. He'd lost enough in his life; he didn't need to add death to his list of sacrifices.

"After an unfortunate delay, it's time to introduce the participants in this quarter's Sector Series. This will be an epic fight today, folks. I've watched these three contestants practice, and I'm confident you'll be entertained.

"From the West Sector, I give you Aidan. He's an aggressive fighter with amazing sword skills. In addition to the sword, he swings a mean mace. Representing the East Sector is Ling; her style of fighting is more subdued than Aidan's, but I think her skill with long range weapons will be a challenge to her opponents. Her expertise with a bow and arrow is unparalleled, and she can throw her spear far and with uncanny accuracy. And last, but of course not least, fighting for the North Sector is Jordan. He's another aggressive fighter who likes to use his shield both as a weapon and for protection. He uses a broad sword to slash at the other players. All three of you take a bow now; all the sectors are watching, make them proud!"

The applause machine played fake clapping from invisible fans.

The referees nodded toward the three. There were no cheering crowds; the only people allowed to witness the event live were the announcer, the referees, and teammates watching from their dressing rooms. During the first Sector Series match there was an audience. The organizers quickly realized it wasn't a good idea after members of the audience started yelled warnings and locations of their opposing team. Cheating was not to be tolerated, and although those audience members had been reprimanded, the government felt it was better to cut off the opportunity entirely.

Aidan and Ling stood toe to toe, staring into each other's eyes. They both knew only one of them would be left standing at the end of their match. The players clutched their weapons of choice, trying to hide the fear invading their minds and bodies.

Contestants were required to learn every rule of the Sector Series, but the referee had to go over the four main rules:

1. This is a fight to the death.

2. No other team member may assist the fighter.

3. Anything you find in the arena may be used as a weapon.

4. If the winner is unable to leave the arena, their victory is forfeited.

The referee blew a whistle, signaling to the players they had ten minutes before the fight commenced.

Aidan had a sword in one hand and a mace in the other. If he was going to die, he wanted it to be up close, looking into the eyes of his opponent. Not a vicious person by nature, he'd learned to be callous about the inherent violence of the Sector Series by not letting himself turn away while watching his teammates fight, and sometimes die. The first death he witnessed pierced his soul. He threw up and had to lean on a wall. After that experience Aidan became more and more numb. As the team captain, he could show no weakness. Before every match he had the team recite a mantra.

"We are bold. We are bold!"

He wished that were true.

Aidan hadn't observed where Ling went; he'd been too focused on his strategy, but he was still surprised she wasn't standing in front of him. Panic replaced his boldness. He needed to regain his confidence somehow, but Aidan found he couldn't bring himself to move. When he realized Ling didn't want to fight up close, he didn't know what to do. He wished he'd watched her training videos. All the other players fought the same way he did. This would be his first fight against someone he couldn't see.

Calm down. Think! Get out of the open. She could be aiming at you right now!

"I must be bold! I must be bold!" he yelled to the sky.

Aidan looked for cover. The nearest thing he could hide behind was a large boulder on the edge of the clearing. Running a zigzag pattern to avoid being hit by one of Ling's arrows, he made it to the rock unharmed. Catching his breath, Aidan scanned the trees, looking for his opponent. He couldn't think of her as a person, only as his target. It made it easier for him to pretend he was playing a video game.

There. A flash of light in that tree. It must be her spear.

Ling ran to the cover of the nearby trees. She knew a hand-to-hand battle would be her undoing. She found herself feeling thankful her coach had forced her to watch all those hours of fighting videos. Her strength was in her spirit, not her body. She'd never had a reason to build her strength before this event. Now her best weapon was her mind.

Ling chose to fight from afar. In her right hand, she grasped a ten-foot spear. Slung across her back was a quiver of arrows and a short bow. Her team captain had attempted to toughen her up, but she'd refused. Not caring about the deaths of her opponents was unacceptable to her. Live or die, she had to honor the lives of those she fought against. Her hand to her heart, Ling patted the photo of her parents hidden under her vest.

She was ready.

Ling climbed into a pine tree at the edge of the arena.

A player could fight from anywhere, either at close range with their opponent or from a distance. Waiting would be her first strategy. Hoping it would unnerve Aidan, she leaned back on the limb and watched him. Ling wished she didn't know his name; it made this too personal. Killing a stranger might be easier for her.

Then Ling saw Aidan's head turn in her direction and knew she'd been spotted. Disappointed by the swiftness of her discovery, she jumped down from the tree and ran farther into the forest. It couldn't end this soon. She felt panic as she ran and tried to stifle the feeling by planning her next move.

Father, Mother, what should I do? I don't want to die. I want to come home to both of you. Send me your strength.

Ling stumbled on a tree root and fell into a dip in the forest floor.

Just like every female in a movie, she thought with disdain. *Why can't my failure be more original?*

Refusing to lose, she sat up but stopped. She remembered one of her favorite bedtime stories about a tiger trap. A resourceful hunter sharpened bamboo and stuck the spears into a ditch, then covered the trap with leaves. The unsuspecting tiger, a man-eater, fell into the trap and died. Ling wondered for a moment why this was her favorite story but was thankful it came to mind now. She would become the tiger trap. This would be her only chance for victory.

If she couldn't fight from a distance, she would become Death.

Chapter 13

February 8, 2111

Pete looked at his clock at the conclusion of the first match, shocked at its brevity. These fights usually lasted hours, but this time it was over in under an hour. He felt a bit cheated by the show. If the next match ended this fast, he didn't know what he'd do for the rest of the evening.

"Well, that was a short match," said Pete. "Pity about the girl. Wanted her to win. Can't wait for the next battle. Poor kid only has one hour to recover before facing the North's finest. Think I'll take a stretch then settle in for the spectacle."

Pete often spoke out loud. It helped him feel less lonely, a state he would admit only to himself. It was on nights like these he really missed his wife, Jean. Her stubbornness, her independence, her intelligence. Those three aspects of her personality, the ones Pete loved most, had killed her.

They'd been married for twenty-five years BIB. For the most part it was a good marriage, with a few bumps that all long-term relationships encountered. Pete often told her he'd be lost without her. To which she'd reply with her canned response, "Where am I going?"

Once the devastation of sleeplessness began, she refused to earn pills. Jean remained convinced, all the way up until the evening she passed away, that there was some sort of conspiracy going on, and she refused to take part in it.

"Pete, I can't in good conscience work for a government that enslaves their citizens," she'd said. "Why won't President Grieves tell us what's happening? And why isn't anyone working on a cure for us?"

Pete couldn't answer her. He was the type of person who didn't have deep thoughts. He enjoyed life and loved his wife. BIB, he liked to watch football and drink beer. A simple life was enough for him.

"You know I tried, Pete." And she had, at least at first. They went to the Great Hall together when the madness began, and she looked at the lists of tasks and chose to farm. She loved gardening and figured that would get them Somnum and she could enjoy herself at the same time.

"And you enjoyed it, Jean. So why the change?"

Pete tried not to sound desperate, but couldn't help himself.

"For a while it was good enough, until I started thinking about our situation. Really thinking about it. I know there's something wrong with the way we're all being forced to live. I heard rumors about what goes on in the Capitol. Some say they all sleep and live in regular houses, not these tiny pods. Whispers about the cause of our sleeplessness are disturbing. So I ask you again, why won't President Grieves tell us what's happening?"

"I'm sure she will when the time is right. If we can't trust our government, then we've lost. They would never lie to us. Until then, we need to earn sleep. There has to be a task you'd be willing to do, Jean. Please, do it for me. I don't ask you for much, but now I'm begging you."

"Pete, I love you and would do anything for you. Except this. It's not about the tasks; it's about not knowing the why of everything. If the citizens don't take a stand, all is lost. What kind of life would we have if we just followed orders blindly? Why should any of us accept the way things are without question? I'm better than that. *We're* better than that. Pete, try to understand."

Pete's eyes filled with tears. Instead of wiping them away, he let them roll over his cheeks and drip off his chin. He felt helpless against Jean's determination.

"Jean, what's wrong with staying alive to fight? You can't find the truth from the grave. All you'll accomplish is devastating me."

She sighed. "Hold my hand, Pete. Let's not fight, not about this, not now. You know I'm stubborn. I want our last days together to be a pleasant memory for you. Let's reminisce about the wonderful days BIB. We were such a good couple, weren't we?"

On day three of Jean's refusal to work for sleep, Pete traded a bottle of his homemade liquor for an extra batch of pills. He brought the precious packet of Somnum pills home to offer to his wife. The look on her face when she realized what he'd done broke his heart. She'd looked appalled, not thankful. He knew she'd refuse to take the pills. He'd failed to save his wife.

During Jean's protest, Pete thought she was being paranoid, but now he wondered if that was true. After a week without sleep, his wife died. She left him alone to face a bleak future.

The first two months after Jean's death, he mourned for his loss. In the days that followed, Pete railed against the tired new world. He wouldn't accept the loss of his wife. Sadness morphed into bitterness, his loving nature turned into cynicism. Today he wasn't the Pete that Jean loved, the gentle giant that was her loving husband. There was little chance she'd recognize the curmudgeon he'd become.

After that, he resented her. Resented that she'd left him behind without thinking about him. Her protest wasn't noble; it was selfish. Pete understood Jean's wish to make a stand, but to this day he could not fathom why that was more important than their relationship. He still felt they could have fought against the government together, found out what was going on, and done something about it. Gradually, he felt his love slip away, leaving a hole in his heart he knew would never be filled again.

After that, Pete had difficulty trusting anyone. To him everyone was a liar, always looking out for themselves. Yet he knew that wasn't really true about his Jean. But he also knew that he couldn't forgive her for leaving him so desperately alone.

"It's your fault I've become the man that I am today!" he screamed one day at her photo. "I'm mean, I cheat, and I can't remember what happiness feels like." Pete resisted the temptation to throw his wife's photo against the wall of his pod. Something told him he would regret that action later.

Instead he opened one of his bottles of liquor and took a long drink, knowing his nightly binge-drinking session was the only way to get through his existence. No one else knew he drank every evening. He wished that would be enough to go to sleep but this strange plague that affected him and the rest the citizens wouldn't allow such a simple solution. The alcohol relaxed him, though, and he knew it was a ritual he couldn't do without. Pete walked around to the back of his pod and checked on his still to be sure his next batch was brewing. Then he checked the supply of vegetables and fruit, the main ingredients for his liquor. He had enough for now.

Then Pete did the only other thing that relaxed him—he counted his stash of sleeping pills. Satisfied he had enough for now, he put away his illicit treasures. His side business had become a reality after that first trade for Jean: liquor for pills. Realizing there would be a market for extra sleep, he used the tragedy of Jean's death for gain. He knew it was an ironic twist that both his job and his side business was to dole out the very thing that would have saved his beloved if she hadn't been so determined.

His Jean.

Chapter 14

February 8, 2111

Aidan lay on the table in his team's arena dressing room. His remaining teammates cleaned him up, massaged his arms and legs, and tried to get him to relax. He was still in shock from the loss of his ring finger during his match with Ling. When he fell into her trap, her spear sliced off his finger. Furious, he'd tried to wrench the spear from her hands, but a sudden renewal of strength fortified her arms. In the end, he used leverage to pry the spear from her. It was at this point she appeared to give up. Piercing her heart with his sword had been easy while experiencing the adrenaline of losing his finger.

But once the adrenaline wore off, he couldn't stop the rush of guilt.

One teammate bound his hand while trying to keep the remaining fingers and thumb free; Aidan needed them to hold his mace. All Aidan wanted to do was sleep, but he knew that was impossible. He needed to regain his strength and ready himself for the next fight.

One of the referees came into the room with a fifteen-minute warning until the next match, turned around, and left without further comment. For a brief moment, Aidan considered giving up during the next fight, letting his opponent kill him, and greeting what he imagined was the sweet relief of death. Instead he gathered his courage and began the team cheer.

"We are bold! We are bold!"

The team cheered along with him, seemingly encouraged by the burst of energy from Aidan, confident that their captain would win this next match. If he did, it meant victory in the Sector Series.

Aidan rose from the table and went over to a washbasin to splash cold water on his face, took another deep breath, and said, "I'm going to win." The last part was said in a whisper so he was the only one to hear it. Not wanting to disappoint his teammates by appearing timid, he straightened up and walked with false courage to the table and lay down for the last few minutes of precious rest and reprieve from what was ahead.

As in the previous battle, the two contestants lined up toe to toe in the center of the arena. Aidan held his sword in his right hand and his mace in his mangled left hand, staring intently into the eyes of his opponent, Jordan. His opponent stared back with equal intensity, never breaking eye contact. Aidan's breathing was jagged, Jordan's deep and measured.

Jordan had a sword, and in his other hand he gripped a shield with a spike in the center of it, his lips puckered in concentration.

The referee wished them both good luck and told them they had ten minutes until the start of their match. This time, unlike the previous match, no one ran away. They circled each other while looking around for possible places as areas of defense. Neither lost eye contact with their opponent for more than a brief moment.

Looking into Jordan's eyes, Aidan imagined he saw Ling's eyes instead. He blinked several times to rid himself of the vision. Aidan was the last thing she'd seen before he stabbed her in the heart. Now he couldn't erase the memory of her face.

Once ten minutes passed, the referee shouted, "Your match has begun, fight for the glory of your sector!"

Jordan struck first, with the assurance of a winner and the hope that Aidan was still exhausted from his first fight. He was right. Aidan was slow to react and the sword bit into his left bicep. He mounted another assault on the left side of his body. The pain sent him into shock, and he stood there, not making his move. Jordan smiled, not with pleasure, but with the hope this might be a quick match. Jordan had promised his family he would win and was determined not to fail. He was as proficient a fighter as his opponent and wanted to prove that to himself and to everyone watching on vidscreens in their pods. Jordan's family told him they'd be watching. He practiced for hours using his shield and was skilled in utilizing it for both protection and as a weapon. Jordan hoped Aidan realized that he was outskilled.

Jordan raised his sword to strike Aidan again but was surprised to hear a loud clanging as Aidan hit Jordan's shield with his sword. The reverberation shook all the way down Jordan's left arm. He looked at Aidan in disbelief. Jordan's confidence drained from him, and his face turned white.

Those precious few seconds of Jordan's immobility created enough time for Aidan to gather his wits and prepare for the continuation of the match. Holding his breath, he raised his left arm, swung the mace over his head, and yelled, "I must be bold! I must be bold!"

The mace hit the spike on Jordan's shield and bounced away, tearing at the flesh on his face. The move served its purpose—Jordan backed away to gain a better position. Aidan's confidence grew as he moved forward and Jordan backed up, matching him step by step until Jordan was up against a tree. Aidan swung the mace, piercing the shield and knocking it out of Jordan's shaking hand.

Jordan swung wildly with his sword, missing Aidan over and over. At last the sword connected with

Aidan's right leg. A rage unknown to Aidan erupted from deep within him, smashing what was left of his empathy.

"You dare to rip victory from me!" The words were yelled with such power, spittle dotted the face of his opponent.

The force of this hatred spewed at him from a stranger seemed to paralyze Jordan. He dropped his arms and stood there waiting.

Aidan took a step back and then plunged his sword into Jordan's heart. Jordan slumped down and was dead before he hit the ground. Aidan pulled the sword out and dropped it on the dirt. He couldn't stand the feel of it and didn't want to touch it ever again.

The referees quickly declared Aidan the winner of the Sector Series. He didn't bother to acknowledge his victory, and he limped with great effort toward his dressing room.

The loudspeakers filled with the cheers of spectators not present. False applause for a hollow victory. The sounds filled Aidan's head, further confusing his emotions. He looked up at the enormous vidscreen filled with hundreds of images. A computer-generated crowd happy for the winner. Aidan noticed they all had the same face. His.

As he was leaving the arena he thought: *Why doesn't this feel like a victory?*

Chapter 15

February 9, 2111

As hard as she tried not to think about it, not being the one to do the cleaning this time meant that Kate had lots of time to think about the corpses. The young people who'd died in the name of a state-sanctioned sport. Kate had told Decker she knew nothing about the losers, but she'd lied. And she didn't understand why she did. She'd wanted to know about the players this time and watched some of the post-tournament coverage. Watching an actual tournament live would never be an option for her; the violence would crush her. Her mind brimmed with the scenes of previous cleanups; she had no room left to add scenes of the fights. If she'd known her next assigned job was going to be a cleanup, Kate wouldn't have watched.

Turning on the news the night before, she sat in front of her vidscreen and watched a show about the biographies of the two people who'd lost. The perky female newscaster, whose name Kate didn't bother to remember, talked about the history of the Sector

Series and then named the winners from the past years as their names scrolled across the screen.

After the preliminaries, the newscaster talked about the short lives of Ling and Jordan, and a slideshow played on the screen behind her—a slideshow of various photos of the two contestants from birth until age sixteen, the minimum age of the participants in the Sector Series.

Kate felt nauseous, resisting the urge to turn away from the spectacle.

The contestant from the East Sector, Ling, was an only child who spent her time taking care of her parents. She was a tall, thin Asian teenager with long black hair. A shy girl, Ling didn't have the time or the desire to make friends. She'd been a late-in-life child, arriving when her mother was forty-eight, the love of her adoring parents' lives. Ling's mother now suffered from a form of debilitating rheumatoid arthritis and had to use a wheelchair full-time. Her father had a heart condition; he wasn't able to take any jobs to earn sleep for the family. So when the opportunity arose to volunteer for the games, Ling signed up without a second thought.

During the first year of sleeplessness, there'd been talk about a draft system to get contestants for the Sector Series. It turned out there was no need because the prize—an unlimited number of sleeping pills—was an immediate attraction to the most desperate.

Families like Ling's, where only one person could

work to earn pills, needed that prize. Once the volunteers from each Sector applied, a computer chose the contestant at random. The applicants avoided thinking about the death aspect of the Series, only of the prize.

Jordan, the contestant from the North Sector, came from a family of four children, of which he was the eldest. He was a tall, athletic guy with shaggy blond hair, and he had the look of a Viking. Although there were no health issues in his family, the need for the pills was just as urgent as in Ling's family. His parents didn't want his younger siblings, aged two, six, and nine, to perform the tasks necessary to earn sleep. None of the tasks were geared for children. It was up to Jordan and his parents to earn enough sleep for the entire family. He took this responsibility upon himself, telling the interviewer that his parents wouldn't have asked him to make such a sacrifice.

There was now a law set by the President that no family could have more than two children, but Jordan's youngest sibling had been conceived a few days before the new law. Back then, the government hadn't been draconian enough to force anyone to give up their babies. The law proved unnecessary. Once the population realized the near impossibility of raising more than one or two children, the problem took care of itself. Large families were a rarity within the Nation, and if things according to plan, would soon become extinct.

Thinking the broadcast was finished; Kate moved

to turn off the vidscreen. She froze when she heard the newscaster say there was footage of the parents coming up next.

No! They wouldn't be that callous!

But sure enough, there was a photo on the top right of the screen. Angered at what she perceived as taking advantage of grieving parents, Kate moved again to turn off her vidscreen. Then she heard the voice of Ling's mother and couldn't switch it off. She felt compelled to watch.

"Ling was a gentle girl," said the mother. "Good student. Good daughter. Respectful to us. I miss her smile and her laughter."

The reporter turned to Ling's father.

"Is there anything you'd like to add to your wife's comments?"

Ling's father looked past the announcer to a point on the wall of the television studio. Stoic.

"Sir?" prompted the reporter.

"My Ling was a flower. She was pure goodness. She showed much honor to her parents. She didn't deserve to die."

Ling's father stroked his wife's hand in a vain attempt to comfort her, but it was apparent she was still agitated. He murmured to her in Cantonese, then stilled his hand and spoke again.

"I, we, do not understand why she entered this contest. She told us she wanted to help, to honor us, but this is wrong. We struggled, but we were together.

Now Ling is gone and we won't sleep again. We refuse to sleep. Our life is over without our flower."

"Do you mean you are choosing to die?" asked the reporter.

"We want to join Ling. There is no life without our daughter. Please respect our wishes and leave us alone."

The newscaster turned to the camera. "Well, folks, this is a new development. I can't recall any other parents choosing to die due to the outcome of the Series. Could this be a new trend? What do you think of this? Vote now on your vidscreens! Should parents be allowed to die if their child loses? Press 1 for yes, and 2 for no. Don't forget the new comments feature. If you'd like to leave a comment, press 3. I'll report the results at the end of this broadcast."

The show cut to the next interview, which appeared to be taking place at the family's doorstep. Jordan's parents looked numb and shocked. His father's face was red, displaying his outrage at this interview.

"And you, sir, what would you like to say about your son Jordan?"

"Last night my wife lit a candle and said a prayer for Jordan. We are grieving, please leave us alone."

"But, sir—"

"Our son has just died! What kind of monster are you?"

"Sir, the viewers want to know more about the brave young man who gave his life for the glory of the North Sector."

Jordan's mother stared at the reporter, refusing to speak.

"Jordan was a good son. He was funny, smart, and sweet. My wife and I understand why he volunteered, but we are still shocked by his death. We expected him to win because he told us he would. Now we don't know how we'll go on. We never expected to be in this situation."

"I do want to say something," said Jordan's mother. "He was my baby, my oldest child, the joy of my life. The only reason he participated was to help his family. Jordan is... was... a kind boy. This barbaric game..."

"That's enough," said Jordan's father. He turned back to the camera. "You're getting her all worked up! She has high blood pressure. We've already lost one family member, now please go."

Jordon's mother sobbed as the door slammed.

The announcer turned toward the camera. "Well, there you have it. Everything you wanted to know about the brave contestants and their families. Now for the results of the poll. Seventy-five percent of you think parents should be allowed to die. There aren't any comments. I have to say, those aren't the results I was expecting. Tune in next week when we interview the winner of the series, Aidan from West City. I'll bet his sector is grateful for that amazing young man."

Chapter 16

February 9, 2111

The Sector Series began with bi-monthly events that culminated in the finals every year. Each sector played six matches a year. Part of the winners' reward was for their sector to stay out of the next year's series. That, and bragging rights.

Each team was comprised of six members, and the team drew lots to determine the order in which they fought. At the end of the series, the team with the most members left alive won. In the event of a tie, the referees used the voting feature on the vidscreens.

This year North, East, and West were playing, and the citizens of the South Sector reveled in their yearlong reprieve. Their team practiced, watched the current matches, and hoped to win when they would be forced to play again the next year. Last year's winning team had four players alive at the end of the series. Miguel, voted the captain by the other three because their original captain died, watched the current series with interest. He wouldn't be required to take part again; his duty now was to train the next series' players.

Decker was trying to figure out the best way to clean up the mess left over from the latest fight. Some called them games, others tournaments; he'd once heard a group of guys call them epic battles. He thought of them as cruel spectacles.

There was no simple way to clean up the bodies. Decker hoisted them up one at a time and placed them in a copper vat located at the far end of the arena. Good fighters tended to be tall and muscular. Great for sport, but a pain to carry. Decker wondered how Kate did this without help. He smiled briefly, knowing she'd offer to kick his ass for insinuating she was a weak, helpless female. He wouldn't let himself imagine her doing this task; she wasn't meant for this dreadful work. No one was.

Tossing the second body into the vat, it landed face up. Decker stared at the bloody face, her sightless eyes hidden under swollen eyelids. Decker tried to avoid looking at the faces—that was the one part of them that came back to him when he slept.

On those nights, he wished he couldn't dream.

Returning to the bloody site where he'd removed the bodies, Decker looked for pieces that remained behind. Errant toes, ears, or other parts hacked off during the fight had to be added to the vat. Yesterday's game was more brutal than the norm; he found bits and pieces belonging to all three participants. He wondered if the winner would miss his left ring finger. Decker looked for a large leaf to serve as a glove for picking up the fighter's bits.

Next chore: erase any sign of the gore. First, he added more dirt from the pile at the far end of the arena. The huge wheelbarrow intended for this leaned against a mountain of dirt. It took three trips back and forth to soak up the blood and gore. With each trip, Decker whistled in a failed attempt to make it seem like an everyday, ordinary task.

Decker stopped to wipe his brow and consider the insanity of the task. Sanctioned murder as a sport, and here he was cleaning up after it. The Decker of ten years ago would've been shocked. Disgusted and shocked. He wondered if trying to become numb would be good for him, then rejected that notion. Like Kate said, if he ever stopped feeling bad about senseless death, he would disappear and become someone he wouldn't want to know.

He dumped the final load on the ground and raked the dirt, forming a design required by the government—an intertwining logo representing the four sectors. To Decker the design looked like a four-leaf clover. He couldn't help himself, he laughed. He didn't think it was funny. No, it was ironic.

"Not very lucky to end up here," Decker said to the empty arena.

Before he finished, he murmured a few words over the bodies. It wasn't a prayer; he'd never set foot in any type of religious building. Decker felt the dead players deserved more respect. When he finished with his ceremony, Decker looked over at Kate. She remained with her back to him, leaning against the tree. Her shoulders were shaking; he could tell she was crying.

Reaching for the copper knob above the vat, he turned on the lye dispenser and cranked up the heat. There were two choices for disposing of the bodies. Boiling lye or building a bonfire. He chose fire once and couldn't do it again. Whenever Decker disposed of these bodies, he wished their families didn't have the option to sign over the corpses to the government. He thought they should take care of their loved ones themselves. Decker wondered if the families were rewarded with extra Somnum. It took days for the smell of burning flesh to leave his nostrils and his mind. Eating animals he caught near his camp wasn't an option for weeks. And when he did return to adding meat to his meals, he had to keep his eyes averted from the plate.

The next cleaning crew would empty the copper vat, crushing the remaining bones and teeth. That, and cleanup, were considered choice tasks amongst the non-sleepers because they earned 1.5 times more Somnum pills. That is, as long as you could stomach it.

Decker found out the bone meal was used to fertilize the strawberry plants. That made sense. Strawberries from the Nation were the biggest he'd ever seen. He assumed workers on the farms didn't ask where the fertilizer came from, but they had to have at least suspected. Yet in the end, they probably didn't want to have it confirmed.

It was easier to accept the end product as long as it produced something useful. Decker's discovery of the real use of the bone meal motivated him to stay out of the system. He'd considered moving to North City and pretending he was a non-sleeper to be closer to Kate, but after weighing the pros and cons, he knew staying with the other Sleepers outside of the city was a better choice.

He looked down at the vat with distaste. Fire was faster, but boiling lye concealed the odor of death.

As he was finishing the cleanup, Decker noticed someone, or something, watching him from the bushes.

"Hey, do you need something?"

No reply. The bushes rattled. He thought it might be a squirrel or some other small animal, but called out again in case it was someone spying on him.

"Whoever you are, I'm enjoying this beautiful day not doing anything else. Some girl just cleaned up the mess from the Sector Series. She was here a few minutes ago."

"Ha! That's a lie," said a voice from the bushes.

"If you're going to accuse me of lying, at least say it to my face. Who are you?" said Decker.

A tall young man with blond hair stepped into the light and walked toward Decker. He was favoring his left hand, which was bleeding through a bulky wrap. His bruised face was cast downward as he limped over.

Decker's eyes widened. "You're from the games."

He nodded. "My name is Aidan. I won yesterday for my team." Aidan unwrapped his hand. It was missing its ring finger. "Don't I look like a winner to you? This is my trophy."

"Whoa. So that was your finger I threw into the vat of lye a few minutes ago?" said Decker. "Sorry, I didn't think you'd come back for it. I'd offer to get it back for you, but the lye's already dissolved it."

Aidan laughed, then shuddered. "Yeah, that's not why I'm here. Still can't believe I killed two people yesterday. Kinda wanted to see this place again to make sure it was all real. I noticed you were cleaning and wanted to watch. I didn't think about who would have to clean up my mess. Feels like I should apologize to you."

Aidan stepped closer to Decker, who nodded at him.

"Never thought about the cleaners before. Most of my family chooses jobs working in the food factory. Me, I pick up garbage, or I used to, anyway. When I was twelve, it was my first job. I'm not proud of it, but after seeing what you've gotta do, I think I'll tell my family there's nothing wrong with garbage hauling."

Another hollow laugh from Aidan. Decker looked back toward Kate to see if she was still turned around. She was.

"So, hey, Aidan, if you could keep the cleaning thing to yourself, I'd really appreciate it. I'm not the one that's supposed to be doing this today. I'm uh, helping out a friend."

Aidan looked past Decker and spotted Kate.

"Who's the girl? Is that your friend? Your girlfriend?"

Decker tried blocking his view, but Aidan was persistent. Decker shrugged and moved out of Aidan's way. He didn't see the sense in blocking her anymore.

"Does it matter? Just don't tell anyone you saw me doing this instead of my friend, okay? We good?"

Still staring at Kate, Aidan considered his answer. He waved Decker away.

"Can't tell on you if I don't know your name, buddy. So maybe you and your friend should just go and leave me alone."

"Don't have to tell me twice! Thanks, Aidan."

Decker jogged back to Kate without looking back. Concerned Aidan might change his mind, he wanted to get away.

Chapter 17

Aidan watched as Decker ran to Kate, wondering what their story was. Why would anyone clean up bodies when they didn't have to? The pain in his hand reminded him why he was there. Aidan walked to the spot he'd killed Ling, then to the place Jordan breathed his last.

He looked around at the empty arena, and before he knew it, the tears were flowing. Then the crying turned to sobbing, his body shaking with guilt and grief. It took him several minutes to regain control of himself. Aidan wiped his eyes with the back of his hand, then sat on the ground next to the logo the cleaning guy had created in the dirt. He used his forefinger to trace the outline of the logo.

How was he going to face his family and his friends back in his sector? How could he return as the conquering hero when all he felt like was a murderer? No, he wasn't a murderer. What he did during the match was not illegal in the eyes of the law of the Nation, he was just a killer.

But he had still killed two innocent people to win; there was no escaping that fact. Aidan repeated that to himself for a minute. He'd killed two innocent kids to win a tournament.

He'd looked into Ling's eyes right before he stabbed her with his sword. Watched the life drain from her eyes, saw her mouth go slack, heard her breathing cease. She fought hard, but not hard enough. She seemed to accept the fact that she would lose and relaxed at that last moment. His final blow was met with no resistance. At the time, Aidan couldn't understand why Ling stopped fighting. She still had a chance. Ling had sliced off his finger; he was bleeding heavily. And yet she didn't take advantage of his injury. Now, sitting in the quiet arena, he understood how choosing death might be preferable to being a winner of such a pointless fight. Giving up sounded good to him.

Jordan fought with more fierceness until the end. He and Aidan had similar fighting styles, both brandishing swords, both fighting close. Aidan had to use his mace to dent the shield Jordan used to protect himself. After several attempts the mace pierced the shield, allowing Aidan to fling it away. Jordan died in the same way that Ling did, with a sword thrust through his heart.

After each victory, Aidan felt nauseous. Aidan thought he'd prepared for the violence after watching so many fights on vidscreens, but now he knew that was impossible. He wasn't meant to be a cold-blooded killer. Even if he watched a thousand fights, his true nature would win. Aidan was a kind person, not a fighter.

He stood up and smeared the section of the logo on the ground representing the West Sector and walked out of the arena. He knew he could never go home. Couldn't stomach being celebrated for killing. He needed to get away. He couldn't give up and he didn't want to live the life forced on him because of his sleeplessness.

Aidan needed to think. Was he really, truly committed to leaving the Nation? He sat on top of the mound of dirt on the far end of the arena and thought about his options. His victory guaranteed his family sleeping pills for the next year and also kept West City out of the Sector Series until the year after. Both of these were good things. Guaranteeing peace of mind for his family and sector was the only decent result of this travesty. Aidan kept that thought foremost in his mind.

He couldn't remember anyone in his family ever doing anything violent. They were a quiet, religious family, who went to church on Sundays and performed good works. He'd never been in a fight at school or hurt anyone physically or emotionally. His mother was a gentle woman who stayed home BIB raising her family and taught them her wisdom. His father made his money as a carpenter BIB.

They were a traditional family in some senses but

in others not. Both parents were equal in guiding the family and neither wanted their children to suffer. He knew his parents understood what the Sector Series was, and they knew it would be about fighting. They would still be shocked by the fact Aidan was now a killer. His family knew he was participating, but the reality of what it involved didn't occur to them. The last thing his father said as Aidan left for the competition was, "Have fun!" His father must have been in denial; he'd watched the Series and knew what was involved. He feared his younger sister and brother would be afraid of him. They'd never feared him before, but now, how could they not? Knowing their older brother had taken two lives away changed everything. Aidan could picture his siblings staying just out of his reach, looking at him when he was turned away. Wondering. Trying to find the brother they thought they knew and loved.

Aidan kept seeing the faces of Jordan and Ling in his mind. Ling's choice at the end confused him. Did she realize she was about to lose or was it a matter of not wishing to go on? Was the idea of having to fight in another tournament too much for her? Or was she willing to leave this earth and find whatever peace came after by making an irreversible decision?

Aidan got up and walked the perimeter of the arena again, reliving both battles. It wasn't an intentional action; he found that as he passed a particular tree or rock, a flash of what happened during his fight would come back. Aidan knew this phenomenon was a form of post-traumatic stress disorder. He went back to the center where the map of the Nation was and wiped away the rest of it. The symbolic gesture felt important to him somehow.

His decision made, he knew his life was no longer here. Whether he would be alone or be amongst others didn't matter; he needed to get away from the craziness and find peace at whatever cost.

According to the President, nothing existed outside of the four sectors. All that was left of the U.S. was contained within a defined area. He needed to find out if that was true. It was as if a veil had been lifted from his eyes. The explanations about why the rest of the country was uninhabitable seemed fabricated. Aidan understood he might just be giving himself false hope, but it was better than the despair he felt.

Rumors had persisted throughout the years about the Sleepers living out there, somewhere in the wilderness. Maybe they would let him join them even though he couldn't sleep. All he knew was he needed to get away from the Nation, a place where no one smiled and no one loved. The only thing anyone seemed to look forward to anymore was the Sector Series, and he now knew the raw and awful truth about it in a way that only a Sector Series participant could.

He could no longer be part of a society that honored such a barbaric ritual.

But before he left town, he had to find that guy who'd been cleaning the arena earlier. Aidan had a feeling the cleaner might know something that would help him. Not because of anything the guy said, but because he'd behaved in a way that wasn't usual.

He was cleaning the gore of the match for someone else. No one did that. Aidan headed to the ITS station, intending to search the city for the cleaner and his female friend. Trying not to feel overwhelmed by his decision, he focused on the best way to find them. The only plan he could think of was riding the ITS until he ran into them. Not the most efficient method, but with some luck he'd be successful.

It was a place to start, and he had nowhere else to go.

Chapter 18

February 9, 2111

Kate's ViGor shot was wearing off. She walked with slow, deliberate effort to the ITS. Afraid she might pass out, Decker offered to carry her, but Kate declined; she wanted to get to the train under her own power. It didn't feel right to have him carry her; he'd just done the cleanup, which was enough. Kate hated to owe anyone, and now her debt to Decker was huge. She could manage this on her own, at least. They stopped twice for her to rest, and at last arrived at the turnstiles and pushed through.

"Decker, who was that guy you were talking to?" she asked once they found a seat.

Decker looked surprised. She'd promised to keep her back turned the entire time they were at the arena.

"Oh, just some nosy guy. No problem, he won't say a thing."

"What do you mean? About the cleanup? Does he know who we are? Oh, Decker, I can't get caught, they'll let me die!"

Her thin shoulders shook as she sobbed. Embarrassed by her tears, she hid her face.

"No, I said don't worry, Kate. He doesn't know our names, and he didn't care about what we were doing. That guy has more important things to worry about. He won the Sector Series yesterday and had a finger hacked off during the first fight. The guy looked like he was about to lose it. His mind, I mean. The guy was pretty freaked out. I don't blame him, do you?"

Kate stopped crying. She hated it when she let her emotions take over. It made her feel weak. She didn't want Decker to think that of her.

"I feel sorry for him," she said. "Can you imagine being part of that bloodbath? I mean, how can anyone win and live with themselves? Did he tell you his name?"

"Yup, his name is Aidan. That's all I know about him."

Kate nodded. She'd seen Aidan's profile on vidscreen, too.

"Didn't ask what Sector he's from and didn't want him to know I don't watch the Series," continued Decker. "He might change his mind about not reporting us if he thought we were rebels."

"Rebels? There aren't any rebels, Decker, what are you talking about?"

"Never mind, Kate. Come on, you can rest your head on my shoulder until we get back to the city."

For once she didn't make a fuss about her personal

space and leaned on Decker's shoulder. She sighed and closed her eyes while Decker stroked her hair.

"Decker, tell me a story. I need to think about something else."

"Instead of a story, how about I talk to you about something, okay? There's a lot you don't know about me, Katie. Kate. Sorry."

Kate opened her eyes and looked up at Decker and he gave her a goofy smile.

"What is it?"

"Something I've been thinking. Whenever I see you, you're stressed out, you're tired, and you don't seem to be happy. There has to be a way to improve your life."

Kate looked surprised. "You've been thinking about me?"

Looking embarrassed now, Decker ran his fingers through his hair, seeming to gather his thoughts.

"Well, I've got something to confess. Sometimes after we part, I don't go home right away. I want to know you're back at your pod asleep. I sneak into town and peek in your window."

"You *what*? You've been spying on me?"

Kate sat up, face red, angry.

"It's not spying, Kate. I worry about you. I care about you. I want to be sure you're safe."

Kate felt uncomfortable about this conversation. She hoped Decker wasn't about to declare his love for her or anything stupid like that. She wasn't ready.

"So anyway, Kate, just let me finish this. You know little about my life outside of our friendship and I've done that on purpose. But now I'm ready to tell you more about me." He paused. "I'm hoping I can convince you to leave North City and come with me."

Kate listened while Decker told her about the other Sleepers and their encampment outside of the city. He told her what their life was like and compared it with how she was currently living. Once he was finished, he waited for her answer, but she just sat there.

"You'll really like the other Sleepers, Kate. There are all sorts of people of various ages and from different walks of life. There's Claudia—she used to be a teacher—and she's our age. She teaches the children in our group, and yeah, there are children—three girls and a boy. Besides teaching, she's great at fixing things, telling stories, and cooking. And then there's Jeremy. He is the one who helped to design and build the Imitator Box. Remember when I slipped and said 'we' designed it?"

"I knew there had to be someone else, Decker. You can't lie to me."

Kate smiled for the first time that day.

"Yeah, well, I slipped up, and at that point I didn't want to tell you more about us. So anyway, this Jeremy guy is very cool, too. He and I both like to run, and we both like to tinker. But he's the scientist. He's the one that came up with the Imitator Box and the software that goes with it. Since I'm an artist, I dreamed up the concept and sketched it. We brainstormed together, but I have to admit the majority of the creation should be credited to him."

"How many people are in your group?" asked Kate.

"Well, there are twenty-four of us, not including the kids. And I say that because when we decide something, it's the adults who vote. The kids belong to one of the other Sleepers named Marion. She discovered that her husband couldn't sleep and knew she had to get her children and herself away."

Kate knew for a long time she wanted to leave the city, but didn't think she had anywhere to go. But now, after hearing what Decker told her about the Sleepers, she felt hope. A feeling she hadn't had in ten years.

"You know what, Decker, it sounds great. But there are so many things to think about. How will I get Somnum pills? Is there room for me to stay there? Will the other Sleepers accept me?"

"I'm working on the important details, most of all the part about you not being able to sleep, so you may have to wait a few more days for me to get it all sorted out. But I promise you, I will figure it out and you will be able to come to us in safety."

"Decker, you're the best. So are you finally going to tell me how to contact you?"

Decker stopped smiling. "You know the answer to that."

"Come on, you just asked me to move in with you. Surely you can trust me on this?"

Decker shook his head. "No, I'll find you. There's no other way to do this now. But don't worry. Just get some rest, Katie girl."

The last part he yelled as he ran away from her.

"I told you not to call me that!" she called after him.

Kate watched Decker go, wishing she could see him more often. She was really struggling lately to keep her feelings for him platonic. Turning away from him, she headed to the city center.

With almost no strength left in her legs, Kate shuffled to the SC reload line. Handing her drive to the clerk, she waited. Lines were a part of everyone's existence. No one complained. For the last ten years, no one had ever known any other way of life.

"Give me your SC," said the clerk.

Scanning the contents of her flash drive to confirm the cleaning, he slid her SC into the sleep credit machine.

"You earned thirty-two red hours or sixteen green hours. Now go to the next line for your pills." He tossed her precious card on the counter, already looking past her for the next worker.

The pill line wasn't long today, but she had to interact with the creepy clerk from earlier in the day. Kate frowned. She didn't know the clerks changed lines. She'd already dealt with this one when she got her assignment, and now here he was working the pill line.

The clerk leered at her then grinned with dark,

decaying teeth. Handing her the coveted packet of red pills, the clerk let his grimy hand linger a moment too long. Kate made a mental note of his name tag: Pete. She vowed to avoid his line whenever possible.

New strength entered her body with the anticipation of sleep. The blessed oblivion of rest. Kate moved to a quiet corner of the Great Hall to dry swallow her little red pill then bounded to her small pod nearby. The Somnum pill took exactly five minutes to work. Barely enough time for her to lie down on her bunk without undressing first.

There were no dreams. Kate never chose to dream.

During her dreamless slumber, Decker watched her through her pod window. He usually snuck into town disguised but had never told Kate until today. He didn't want to endanger her with too much information.

No reason for him to sneak into town except for this—he loved to watch her sleep. It was the only time Kate looked relaxed and happy. He struggled with his feelings for her, never sure if it was love or friendship, but at this point Kate would let nothing happen between them.

So for now, Decker had to accept friendship. He took out the note he'd written that morning and slid it under the door of her pod.

Thirty minutes later, Decker walked out of the city, thinking about the cleanup and its aftermath. He'd lied to Kate when he said it didn't bother him. Every cleanup he'd helped her with stayed with him, preventing him from sleeping peacefully. He had horrible nightmares for days afterwards, but it was still worth it to save Kate from the same fate. Although he knew she chose the red pills, he realized the cleanup stayed with her far longer than it did with him.

It was a small sacrifice for his friend.

Chapter 19

February 9, 2111

Jumping off the subway at his stop, Decker ran the five miles to his place. Running was his favorite form of exercise and it also ensured he wasn't being followed. It had never happened before, but he didn't want to be responsible for leading anyone unwanted into their campsite. It wasn't just a camp—he considered it his home. A compound full of Sleepers trying to figure out how to stay alive.

The small group of twenty-eight waved from their tents as Decker passed them. No one was ever sure if he would return after one of his excursions to the sleepless. There were no secrets in the group—they knew he was helping Kate. Most suspected more than altruism motivated his help, but it didn't matter. Kate was his special friend, and no one wanted him to lose that connection.

Decker pulled back the flap of his tent to grab soap and fresh clothes. He took an hour to scrub away the blood and grit of the cleanup. He had to wash his clothes three times before they ceased emitting the same rotten-meat odor that permeated his skin and hair.

The Sleepers didn't need to ask Decker about the cleanups; they could smell the answer.

"Hey, Decker," said Claudia. "Phew! Another cleanup, huh?"

"Yeah, this is one of those days, Claudia," said Decker.

"Hey, Decker, quit smelling up the place! I'm trying to eat here, dude!" said Jeremy.

He sat down by the community campfire, head in hands, and stared back toward the city, thinking of Kate in her pod. Claudia came over and sat next to him, putting her arms around his shoulders.

"If you need to talk about it, Decker, you know I'm here for you. I'll always be here for you."

Decker didn't answer, knowing she was offering herself and her assistance. He shook his head and remained silent. Other members of their group of Sleepers gathered by the fire near him. Sensing his mood, no one else spoke to him, choosing instead to just sit in camaraderie. They waited for him to speak.

"I've been thinking about something for a long time, and I want to ask all of you what you think of my idea."

The Sleepers exchanged looks, a mixture of concern and curiosity on their faces.

"I told you about my friend Kate and how I help her whenever I can with those disgusting cleanup jobs after the Sector Series."

Groans and nods.

"I don't think she can handle much more. She really needs to be taken away from all the horror that has become part of her life. She told me she'd be willing to work in a food factory but those jobs never open up. So the only way she can get the pills now is to clean up after matches. Or she can travel to the Capitol and do some work there, but that would mean moving far away. Plus, I suspect the Capitol wouldn't be a great place for her to live."

A nod from Claudia and Jeremy.

Someone spoke up from the back. "Sorry, Decker, but how is that our problem?"

Decker looked at the gathered Sleepers and sighed. "Let me tell you about a typical day in the life of a non-sleeper, Kate in particular. Because we separated from them early on, most of you have little idea of how they suffer.

"Kate and the others of the sleepless population are obsessed. Every morning they check their sleep card to be sure they can get a supply of Somnum. If Kate is out of credits or is close to being out, she has to stand in line at the Great Hall and accept an assignment, and once she gets there, she's at the mercy of whoever is at the window. Someone there has got to have it in for her. Anyway, that's the reality for most of the sleepless in the cities. Would any of you want to live that way if you didn't have to?"

"But I heard some of them have regular jobs," said

Claudia. "Why doesn't Kate get one of those? I'm not trying to convince you not to have her join us, I'm curious about her other options."

"Yes, there are some that do, but the rest depend on day jobs. These temporary assignments range from garbage pickup to arena cleanup. The worst is, of course, the arena cleanup, as you all know. When I can help Kate with that, I do. Anyone with any kind of humanity is affected after burning young bodies. The only ones who don't go through this are those able to get work in the Capitol. I've already asked her; she has no intention of moving there. She doesn't want to live anywhere near President Grieves and her associates."

"I don't know how you do it, Decker," said Jeremy. "I'd throw up and have nightmares. Dude, I would stop sleeping, and not for the same reason as those poor sleepless bastards."

"Better me than Kate. To answer Claudia's question about a regular job, they are almost impossible to get. Unless you know someone in the government, they're not available. In the beginning of this disaster, the jobs were accessible to anyone that applied. But once someone got one they never quit. Now the only permanent job with openings is being an escort."

He got a few blank looks.

"You know, prostitution."

"Oh," Claudia said, looking away.

Decker continued for another few minutes, trying to explain to others why he wanted Kate to join them. There were no more questions. Instead the group listened, nodded, and absorbed the information.

Jeremy sat next to Decker and motioned he wanted to speak. "What are you proposing we do for her?" he asked. "We don't know why they don't sleep; we don't know why we do. I want to help, I'm sure all of us do, but you need to tell us what we can do to assist her. And how we can do it without endangering the rest of us. We don't want President Grieves and her henchmen to find us."

The Sleepers murmured their agreement with Jeremy's statement.

"It's pretty simple. I bring Kate back with me, and she joins our community." The protest from the others was immediate.

"Stop!" said Decker. "Before any of you says anything, I know she can't sleep."

"Then how are you going to provide her with Somnum?" someone asked.

"There's a guy in town named Pete, he goes by the nickname of Pill Pete, and he has a bunch of black-market sleeping pills. I'll steal them. Simple as that. He won't report the theft because he'd get in trouble for having them in the first place." Decker looked at the gathered circle of Sleepers, trying to gauge their thoughts.

The Sleepers buzzed at the proposition and talked

it over. Decker could hear arguments for and against, and it all made him nervous. After their discussion they decided it was time for a vote.

Jeremy stood up and moved to the center of the circle and said, "All right, everyone in favor of this crazy plan by our dear friend Decker raise your hands."

No one moved for a few seconds, and then Claudia raised her hand. She didn't like the idea of Kate being at camp, but she wanted to support Decker. Then everyone except for two Sleepers raised their hands, signifying their agreement with Decker's plan.

"I see that two of us are not in favor. Marian and Stephen, do you want to express your concerns?"

Marian gestured toward her children and stood up. "They are my reason. I trust you, Decker, I've trusted you since the first day you accepted me and my family. But the safety of my children comes before loyalty to my friends or this group. I'll reserve judgment of your friend Kate until I get to know her better."

"Thank you," said Decker.

"But know this," she continued. "If I think she's a threat, I will demand she leave. And if you choose her over us, I will leave with my family and look elsewhere for shelter. Being harsh is not in my nature, but motherhood makes me fierce."

Marian sat down to a smattering of applause.

"Marian, I respect your point of view. I've known Kate for ten years and never in that time has she said or done anything I would consider suspect. My pledge to you and the rest of the Sleepers is to put your safety first. If I'm wrong about her, I will remove her from our group myself. Stephen, did you want to have your say?"

Stephen nodded and rose to address the group.

"My reason isn't as noble as Marian's," he said, nodding at her. "I'm worried about our supplies. We don't have extra food or shelter. It would make things more difficult for the group. Would this girl be able to help us hunt? Does she have any skills to contribute? And I don't like the idea of our leader putting himself in danger to steal Somnum for her. Yes, I know I sound like a selfish jerk, but we've survived this long by thinking about what's best for the group and not the rest of the people in the Nation."

"Stephen, I don't think you're being a jerk," said Decker. "You are a practical man. Food is important, so is shelter. I ask you to think about one thing. Where would you be if we didn't allow you to join us four years ago? You *learned* to hunt, and you contribute in other ways I couldn't have imagined when you came to us. Please keep an open mind about this. I've never asked Kate about her specific survival skills. Maybe she'll surprise us. She's smart and I'm confident she'll be able to learn whatever she needs to in order to help. Anyone else want to comment?"

Jeremy looked like he was thinking about something. Decker called on him.

"Come on, Jeremy, I recognize that look. What's up, man?"

"What if she doesn't want to join us? I know you're excited about the possibility, and from the way you're talking you think it's a done deal. But what if she changes her mind once she gets here? Does that mean we'd have to pack up and go? Not trying to be negative here, but maybe we should think more like Stephen and consider the practical aspects of what you're proposing. That's it, nothing else. I do hope she joins us."

A shout of 'hear, hear' from some of the group confirmed to Decker he needed to address this.

"You know what?" said Decker. "I've never considered the prospect of Kate going back. Now *I* sound like a jerk. On the off chance she does, there is absolutely no concern on my part she'd tell anyone about us. She hates the Nation as much as we do. So no, I don't think moving right away because of her would be necessary."

Jeremy nodded. No one else seemed to have anything to say.

"So based on the vote, I will ask Kate to join our community. Also, taking into account the concerns of Marian and Stephen, I will explain to her what being a part of us entails."

The group dispersed, and Decker stuck around to think for a bit. What Jeremy had said worried him. Was it possible Kate would want to go back? Maybe even change her mind? She'd seemed open to the idea. Decker didn't want to think about that and instead focused on his idea to steal Somnum. There had to be a way for him to do it or else his plans for Kate would be impossible. Decker stoked the fire, smiling at the support of his friends. He knew what he was proposing was dangerous, but he also knew he had to get Kate away from the city.

Her sanity and life depended on it.

Chapter 20

February 10, 2111

Kate woke up the next morning to find the note from Decker. No one wrote notes anymore since paper wasn't available. People sent emails, and all money was handled electronically, so this seemed unusual to her. She unfolded the dirty scrap of paper and read a scrawled note from Decker. It said, "Meet me at the ITS station this afternoon at 2 PM. We need to talk." He signed it D.

Intrigued and worried, she went about her day, willing the clock to move faster. He'd never left her a note before, or done anything to make her think there might be a problem in his life. This seemed like a warning of some sort. But then she calmed herself down and decided she was being silly.

The cleaning Decker did for her yesterday had earned her enough red Somnum pills for two weeks of sleep. That gave her breathing room to reconsider the choices in terms of jobs. She promised herself she'd return to the Great Hall and look through the list of jobs to find out if there was something else she could do. Kate vowed she wouldn't have Decker go through that again. Despite what he said to her, she knew he paid a price for the cleanings. Whether it was emotional or physical, it didn't matter.

The ITS station was pretty empty as she approached it just before 2 PM. She walked over to a bench, sat down, and waited. Moments later Decker jogged up to her with his usual huge grin.

"Hey, Kate, thanks for meeting me," said Decker.

"You had me a little worried. You've never sent me a note before. With paper...? How do you still have paper?"

"Never mind about that, I have great news, Kate! My community agreed to let you join us."

"What? Was it unanimous?"

Decker fidgeted with the string on his hoodie, delaying his answer. "Well..."

"Decker?"

"It doesn't matter. Enough of the Sleepers voted yes. It wouldn't do you any good to know how many, and who, voted against you. They're worried about their safety, which is understandable."

"Okay, I won't ask again. I'll try to prove myself to everyone."

Decker smiled. "How long will it take you to pack? I can't imagine you have many possessions. I always see you in the same clothes. Not as fashionable as BIB, right? No black leather mini-skirts?"

Kate elbowed him while trying to hide her blushing face. "I can be ready right away."

"I have a few things to take care of, so plan on meeting me here at 9 PM."

They hugged and parted ways. Kate watched Decker break into a jog as he headed into the city, not away. What was he up to?

After Decker cleaned up the bodies at the arena yesterday, Kate couldn't stop thinking about it, and now, watching him leave, all those thoughts came back. She had a few hours until she was to meet with Decker, so she spent the time doing some research. She wanted to know more about the players. The letters they left for their families would be stored in the library. Anyone could access them. The President thought reading their emotional letters would make the rest of the population feel more patriotic.

Her energy was nearing normal levels, so Kate walked to the library instead of taking the ITS. The building was two miles away, in the center of North City. As she approached, she wondered if she was making a mistake. Would knowing the dead players mess with her mind even more?

The library had an impressive emerald-green door, twelve feet tall with a giant brass knocker. Intimidated by the grand entrance, Kate wanted to turn away and head back to her pod, forget about the letters, and go home. She wasn't sure she should go beyond the door. Instead she steeled herself and moved to the entrance.

The brass knocker was heavy; it took more effort than she expected to lift it. When she let go, the booming sound was deep and echoed through the building. She waited ten seconds and let the knocker drop again. Still no answer.

Should she try to open the door or continue to wait? Maybe she should just leave. It seemed wrong for her to just walk in, but by now her curiosity was piqued. She really wanted to read those letters.

She twisted the doorknob, expecting it to be locked. The knob turned smoothly, and the door opened. She called out to see if anyone was in the building but received no answer. Kate entered.

The room dedicated to the letters was on the second floor. Ten years of tablets filled with letters filled four volumes. One for each Sector. The librarians didn't bother to remove the letters of the winners; they wanted a record of every contestant. Kate sat at a round table and began to read the goodbyes penned by the young fighters. Written while not knowing their futures, pouring their emotions and thoughts on the pages in front of her.

Kate found the girl's letter. Her name was Ling.

Dear Mother and Father,

    As I write this to you, I feel great sadness. I want to win the Sector Series for the glory of the East Sector and for my fellow teammates, but more importantly, I want to win for the two of you. I worry about whether I have the strength within me to do so. I know when I volunteered for this you both opposed my decision, but at the time I felt I had no choice.

Mother, you need more help than I can give you. I love you and want to see you get better, and I hope that if I win, more can be done for your arthritis. If not a cure, at least some way to make you more comfortable than in that rickety wheelchair that you currently use.

Father, with your weakened heart I know that you also depend on me to care for you. It must be difficult for you to watch the world pass you by and feel so helpless. You've given me so much—you've taught me the importance of family, and you helped me learn the value of patriotism and patience.

If you're reading this, I have lost, and I've now gone on to whatever is after death. We were never a religious family, so I don't know what to expect. Is there an empty void? Will we meet again? I hope so, but I'm also worried that death will be the end. I'm worried that if one of the other fighters kills me, the last thing I will see is their face and not your loving ones.

Before I go into battle, I will look at the photo of the two of you on your wedding day in China—my favorite picture. Both of you gazing adoringly *at one another. Mother in her traditional red wedding dress, both of you laughing.*

Years ago, you told me that when you married, neither of you thought that our world would come to this. I'll keep that photo of you in my mind and try my best to win so I can return to you.

I've been told the losers' families will be compensated, and I hope that whatever they give you will be enough to keep you going for many years.

Finally, I want you to know I do this of my own free will because all I've ever wanted to do was repay both of you for being such wonderful and devoted parents. Don't think that I resented having to take care of you over the last couple of years. It's the least I can do for the people who gave me life. Please don't be sad. Just think of me as that chubby, laughing baby you've described to me.

I send you all my love,

Ling

Kate was stunned by the emotions overcoming her. Her own parents had died when she was a toddler, and she'd never had the connection with them that Ling had with hers. Grandmother Bridget did her best to raise Kate, but now, reading Ling's letter, it was as if she had a hole in her heart, one that ached with longing. She missed the parents she never knew and mourned for what might have been. Bridget was also gone, missing for ten years. She moved to the next letter.

Hey Mom and Pop,

I'm supposed to write a letter to you in case I die. There, I said it. I want to start out with the fact that I have no intention of losing, and I'm only writing this because the team captain said we were supposed to. And, well, although I usually don't follow rules, this time I'm forced to.

Gotta say, our team is looking pretty strong. There's no way we're going to lose. Being the 'humble' boy you know as usual. Ha ha. I think I'm the best member of the team. I've been practicing for hours every day and intend to make short work of the player I'm up against.

But... just in case, I want to let you know how I feel about you. Mom, you're an amazing woman. You raised four kids, and we all turned out pretty great, I think. You cooked for us, you sang to us, you taught us values, and dragged us to church every Sunday. Ha ha.

I still remember when you walked me to my kindergarten class and how I wouldn't let go of you. I grabbed so tightly that after school you showed me the tiny marks my fingers made on your hand.

Dad, you showed me what it was to be to be a strong man. You worked hard to provide for a family of six and never complained. In the old days, your job as a construction worker taught me that hard work builds character. Because you never went to school beyond the eighth grade, you wanted me to always be learning. You pushed me to do my homework and were proud of all my accomplishments, no matter how small. Despite your tough exterior, I knew how much you loved us all. I'm proud that you're my father.

Please tell Joseph, Angela, and Ken how much I love them. They can be a real pain but they've also made my life really great. Remind them of the fun we had and let them know all the teasing was because I loved them.

Now for the sad part: if you are reading this, then despite my predictions, I lost. But be assured I'll be watching you from the afterlife and hope you won't be too devastated. I know that someday we will be together again and will rejoice when we're reunited. My greatest wish is that you will never read this letter and that I will come home a conquering hero.

Mom and Dad, please don't cry. Just think of me as your proud son.

Love ya,

Jordan

Kate couldn't hold back her tears. The death of these two had changed from a horrifying cleanup job to heartbreaking reality. She'd seen their bodies from afar, but now all she could do was picture them with their families. Jordan was the type of boy that would be a friend to her. He seemed so happy—a funny, loving guy. And Ling. A dutiful, kind girl trying to help her parents.

Kate swiped the letters closed with a mangled cry. The librarian looked up from her desk but didn't admonish her; she knew what Kate was reading.

Walking home, Kate wished she could call Decker. He would understand what she was going through, but he didn't own a phone, not now or before.

Chapter 21

February 10, 2111

Yesterday when he and Kate were traveling back from the cleanup, Decker noticed a sign in the ITS car.

NEED BONUS SLEEP? CALL 767VJM

The sign had given him an idea. A method to get Kate away from North City sooner than he'd planned. Decker called the number from the library. This was the only time he wished he owned a phone. He was impatient to get started and going to the library from his compound took more time than he wanted to take.

Some guy named Remus answered after one ring and set up a meeting at a friend's pod, giving him his address. The only question he asked Decker was, "Where'd you get my number?"

He didn't seem to know of the ITS sign. When Decker told him about it, Remus muttered, "Damn Pete."

Guy can't be very bright, telling me where his friend lives. Or maybe it's really his pod but doesn't want to let on. Either way, dumb move. He had no idea who Decker was, which was a lucky break.

With some time to spare until his meeting, Decker sought out the farms. One of the things the community needed when they left was a way to grow vegetables and fruit. For now, those few Sleepers who ventured into town stole what the group needed. They all hunted, but being able to grow food would be a bonus. Their current location wasn't conducive to farming—there were too many trees and rocks in the way, and the soil was compacted. They'd already stockpiled enough EnUR-G bars to last six months, but it wasn't sustainable.

He headed to one of the bigger vegetable farms and studied the layout. There was a shed filled with tools and seeds. Peeking in the window, Decker was pleased to see the quantity of seeds. No one would miss the small number of packets he'd steal. Decker wondered for a moment where the packets came from, but dismissed the thought.

It was 3 PM, and no one was in the fields, confirming to him they did their outdoor work earlier in the day. Shaking the doorknob, Decker was surprised the shed wasn't locked. He went inside, found the seeds, and wrote down the types, adding sketches of each variety to refer to later. The artistic part of Decker wanted to stay longer so he could sketch the inside of the shed, but the new, more practical side, thanks to Stephen, told him to be quick. He took one last longing look at all the beautiful seeds and tools and then walked out of the shed, closing the door quietly behind him.

A mile down the road was a fruit farm. Knowing a little about farming, Decker knew the easiest things for the Sleepers to cultivate would be berries. He remembered his mother used to complain about the huge blackberry bushes that threatened to take over their backyard. Decker also remembered the fun he had every summer gathering the berries, eating them until his teeth were stained blue and his stomach ached. On those rare occasions when his mother wasn't playing games on her phone, she'd bake the three of them a pie.

It wasn't the time of year for berries, but he was pleased to observe raspberry and blackberry bushes. Strawberries were pretty easy to grow, so he was sure he'd find some seeds in one of the outer buildings. The shed on this farm was also unlocked. Decker wondered at the lack of security. Inside was another abundance of seeds and tools. The main difference in the shed was a bookshelf filled with manuals on horticulture. This would be useful to the Sleepers, but also something that the farmers would notice, if any of these books were missing. Once again Decker had to resist temptation and rely on his practical side to urge him out of there.

Before putting his tattered notebook back into his backpack, he drew a map of the area for future reference. If he wasn't the one to return to the farms, the map would make it simpler for someone else from his community. Decker wasn't prepared to take the seeds now; it would have to wait until they were ready to leave their camp. The chance of the seeds being missed was small, but being cautious had kept the Sleepers safe so far. After ten years of living in this nightmare, Decker learned it was always better to be patient.

At the assigned time, Decker watched Remus show up. He wasn't what Decker expected. Remus was a short, stout man with greasy dark hair. Thinking of the paintings he used to do and how he liked to portray his subjects as animals, he thought of Remus as a rat. After a few minutes, Remus left, muttering obscenities while looking over his shoulder. Decker suspected the pills were kept in that pod.

Tonight Decker planned to steal as many Somnum pills as he could find. The back window of the pod wasn't locked; it was easy for him to slip in. This was the third unlocked entry he'd encountered. Strange to him, but he hadn't lived in North City, and Decker assumed by now that no one locked anything. After years of living in a big city BIB, Decker still thought doors should be locked. A silly notion from his former life.

Remus, or whoever lived here, had little imagination. There was no attempt at decoration or any sign the occupant cared about his surroundings. He peeked into the bedroom when he heard snoring and saw a man who was not Remus in a Somnum-induced sleep.

That answers the question about who lives here. Some poor man who's been cheated by Remus.

After years of watching Kate sleep, he recognized the breathing patterns of a drugged sleep. These sleep zombies never moved.

The Somnum proved easy to locate. The pills were in battered coffee tins—a green can that used to contain decaf coffee and a red can of regular coffee. Decker thought this was pretty funny and had to stop himself from laughing out loud. The man wouldn't hear him, but there might be someone walking by.

The tins were industrial sized, causing Decker to wonder if this guy used to own a coffee shop. Decker was impressed by the size of the stash. There were hundreds of pills, both green and red. He gathered them up and stuck them into his backpack. He climbed out the window, checked his surroundings to be sure no one was watching, and headed back to camp. Stowing the pills before he met up with Kate was a necessary precaution. If they were caught, being in possession of stolen pills would mean death for him and Kate. She would be considered an accomplice.

Decker spotted Claudia first and ran to her.

"Hey, Claudia, I gotta run. Would you put my backpack in my tent?"

He tossed his backpack to her.

"What's the hurry, Decker? You've been gone all day."

Decker stopped long enough to give Claudia a quick hug.

"Sorry, but I'm on my way to get Kate. I'm bringing her here tonight! Would you make sure there's a place for her to move in?" He moved closer and lowered his voice. "Hey, uh, can you tell B about this? I know I should be the one, but I'm on a tight schedule and need to go now."

Claudia nodded. "Yeah, sure." He couldn't help but notice the pained expression on her face.

Decker knew of Claudia's feelings for him but couldn't return them. He did his best to treat her as a friend and urged her to talk to Jeremy more. How ironic, he thought. So much unrequited love in their small group. The only girl for him was Kate, who for now, and maybe always, was out of reach.

Running back to the ITS, Decker felt elated. Things were falling into place. His dream of moving the Sleepers to a safer place and having Kate join them was coming together. But he kept pushing away a nagging thought: What would happen when Kate used all the Somnum he'd stolen? Thinking long term would paralyze him. There had to be a way to cure Kate, and he and his community would search until they found one. It wasn't just for his friend; he wanted to help the other miserable members of the Nation.

Decker slowed down when he spotted Kate waiting in the agreed upon spot, nodding her head to music.

How could the Sleepers not like her? She would win their hearts and give the community a surge of optimism.

"Kate! Earth to Kate." He touched the top of her head to get her attention.

Kate jumped, then smiled when she saw it was Decker.

"Damn it, Decker, I don't like to be surprised."

"Are you ready? Or I guess the real question is, are you going to come with me to meet the Sleepers?"

"Geez, you sound like you're asking me to the prom! I already said yes, remember?" She squinted at him suspiciously. "Are you having second thoughts about inviting me?"

"Nah, just wanted to be sure. This is a huge step you're taking, Kate. Once you leave, it'll be hard to come back. Someone will notice you're gone, then report you."

"Decker, I said *yes*! Now where do we go?"

They headed to the ITS station. Decker noticed Kate had a small satchel besides her messenger bag. He couldn't help but feel a little sad that her whole life could be packed into two small bags. Then he remembered his entire existence was contained in his backpack. Simpler times.

At the door of the train Decker bowed to Kate. "After you, madam."

She laughed. "You're crazy, and that's one of the things I love about you."

Did she just say love?

Chapter 22

The five miles to the encampment gave Kate and Decker an opportunity to discuss more about her soon-to-be new home.

"I'm getting nervous," said Kate. "Maybe this is a mistake. Stop. Decker, stop!"

Kate couldn't calm down, her palms were sweaty, and she was trembling. She knew Decker wanted her there, but she couldn't forget that two of the Sleepers had voted against her.

"Why are you worried now? It'll be fine. I promised you."

"But what about the two who voted no?"

"Not a problem, seriously," he said. "We talked it out and they're fine with this. They agreed to give you a chance. I won't lie, they'll be watching you, but there isn't anything you'll do to warrant getting kicked out."

Kate wasn't entirely convinced, but she so wanted to take a chance on this. She promised herself to get to know each Sleeper and become indispensable. They continued on to the encampment. Her heart was pounding as they approached the main campfire.

"Everyone, I want to introduce you to Kate."

Each of the Sleepers greeted Kate with a hug and a smile, and with each one, she felt a little better. Some of them asked her questions about her life in the city, but most were silent, aware of how nervous she was.

"Thank you for accepting me," said Kate. "It took a lot of convincing before I agreed to come here. Decker assured me I wouldn't be putting any of you in danger. I hope that's true."

Claudia's smile hid her worry. She stepped forward and offered to get Kate settled into her new home.

"You'll be sharing a tent with me," said Claudia. "I hope you don't mind. There isn't anywhere else for you to live right now."

"Oh, yes, that's very generous of you," said Kate. "Decker tells me you two are close friends. I think that's great."

They walked toward a rickety tent decorated with drawings. Claudia had sketched animals and flowers on it using the coal from their fires.

"Decker has been good for our group," said Claudia. "He's decisive and smart. I can lean on him when I feel hopeless. Did you know he's a great hugger?"

Kate shook her head. A twinge of jealousy hit her.

"Another wonderful thing about him is his art. We have that in common. Some nights by the campfire he tells me about the paintings he used to do."

The way Claudia talked about Decker startled Kate. It took her a bit to pinpoint why. Then she realized Claudia was in love with him. She wasn't sure how she felt about that.

"Once you're settled in, Kate, come back to the fire. We eat together as a community. Unless you're too tired today, then I can bring you your meal."

"I'll be fine, and thanks again."

Jeremy was waiting for Claudia when she exited the tent.

"Do you think she'll fit in?" he asked in a low voice.

Kate could hear them speaking through the thin walls of the tent, despite their whispers.

"She's a nice girl, Jeremy, but I don't know. Kate deserves a life free of the horrors of living in the city, but the Sleepers deserve to live, too. I hope this wasn't a mistake. She might not like the way we live. There's no indoor plumbing or vidscreens here. I wonder if she can adjust?"

"Decker seems to have confidence in her and he's rarely wrong about anything. My trust of his judgment is unshakable. We would both be wise to listen to him. Besides, she seems nice."

"You're right. I need to trust in Decker. And I agree, she seems nice. Maybe we could even be friends."

Smiling, Kate felt happy. Knowing they liked her was a relief. These were good people. Kate sat in Claudia's tent, not quite believing she'd run away.

After hearing the conversation between Jeremy and Claudia, the impact her arrival had on the lives of the Sleepers was made clear to her. She hadn't thought of how she might change their lives or make things difficult. Decker had convinced her life was better among the Sleepers, and she hoped he was right.

Despite what Claudia said, she didn't mind the primitive living conditions—it reminded her of camping as a child. Her concern was for the members of the group and their future. The encampment seemed too close to the city, and it wasn't that hard to get here. What if someone stumbled upon their hideaway? And on top of all of that, relying on Decker for sleeping pills made Kate feel uncomfortable. She owed him so much because of the cleanups he'd done for her. Now he was risking his safety by stealing pills for her. Most likely from that creep, Pete.

"Hey, Kate, how're you doing?" asked Decker. He was standing at the opening of the tent. "Have you unpacked yet? You have everything you need?"

Kate looked around the tent as if taking inventory. She held up her empty satchel as proof of her unpacking.

"Oh, I'm fine, Decker, just getting used to being in a new place. It's comfy in here," she said.

He gave her a look. "What's going on?"

She shook her head. "Nothing. It's nothing. I'm just... I'm really worried that all of you will get caught because of me."

Decker stepped into the tent, then reached into his backpack and pulled out a bulging cloth bag. He handed it to Kate. She opened it and the red and green Somnum pills tumbled out, forming a pile on her bed. There were enough pills to help Kate sleep for at least two years. She looked up at him in shock.

"Decker! You stole these! But from who or where? Please don't say it was from Pete?"

Decker shrugged.

"I knew it! He's the only guy I know of who sells these things on the black market. Decker, this is dangerous! If they catch you, who knows if I'll ever see you again."

"And that's why I am not confirming to you where I got them, Kate," he said. "I got these so you can get a good night's sleep. Every night. No cleanups. Doesn't that sound good?"

She couldn't help it. A smile tugged at the corner of her mouth. "It sounds fantastic."

"Okay, now, there's someone here that says she knows you. Come outside."

They both exited the tent, and Kate looked back into it with a sigh. Her new home. The home she'd be sharing with Claudia.

The flaps on the nearest tent moved and out stepped the last person Kate ever expected to see.

Grandmother Bridget.

Ten years of relief and sorrow rushed through her mind. All the wasted years, all the sadness, all because she thought Grandmother Bridget was dead. Kate ran to her, arms wide open.

"Bridget! Oh, Bridget, I thought you were dead! Where were you? Have you been here the whole time?"

Tears were streaming down Bridget's face as they took each other in. They hugged, neither able to speak for some moments. Decker looked utterly confused.

"You know each other?"

Finally Bridget pushed her away and said, "She's my granddaughter!" She held Kate by the arms. "You're looking good, my girl. I thought you'd died as well. I looked for you when the CDC began the evacuation from the city. Your apartment was a mess, Moongie was crying for you—I thought the worst. Not wanting to give up while things were in chaos, I stayed hidden and continued to watch your apartment for days, confident you would show up. I finally had to make peace with the fact that you were either dead or stuck in the Nation."

"Then what happened?"

"I realized I could sleep, which turned out to be an anomaly. There were still evacuations going on, so I followed a group into West City and observed the surrounding people. Once I discovered I was different, I knew I had to hide. Sleepers were disappearing, and no one knew where they went or if they were still alive. From that day forward, I lived amongst other groups of Sleepers."

Kate looked at her, surprised.

"Yes, there are others. This isn't the only group."

"More groups of Sleepers, Bridget?" said Decker. "That's... that's incredible. Why didn't you tell us this before? Once we leave here, we'll have to find the others. We'll discuss this more as we go."

"This is going to sound silly, but I never thought to mention it to you. I was so happy to find this group; I was tired of moving around. Not that I was ever asked to leave a group, but deep inside, I felt I had to keep moving. Searching. For what, I wasn't sure. Turns out my granny senses were still working. I was searching for Kate without realizing it." Bridget said the last part while smiling up at Kate.

Decker's face was alight with excitement. "We'll have to get you a map. Get you to show us—"

"Decker, I'd like to have some time alone with my granddaughter to catch up. We have ten years' worth of conversations and hugs to get to. Okay?"

Decker laughed. "Would I say no to you? I can't believe this. Yes, you and Kate deserve to have time to yourselves. I'm so glad you two found each other. What are the odds?"

Bridget beamed at Kate. "Yes. What are the odds?"

Remus watched the arrival of the new girl to the community of Sleepers. He recognized her as one of Pete's favorites from the pill and assignment lines. He didn't know her name, but had overheard Pete refer to her as Curly. Pete loved to pretend he had no assignments to give her. Remus wondered why she was in the Sleepers camp and how she'd hooked up with this group. The reunion between the girl and the older woman was another unexpected development. He wondered what the story was. Was the older woman a Sleeper?

Sleepers kept to themselves, it was unusual to see them reveal their true nature to an outsider. At least that was his impression since he'd never met one in the city.

Remus took out his tablet to add to his roster of members, and listed her as 'new girl,' then added a question mark.

Remus had watched Pete and the Sleepers while planning his revenge. This girl might prove useful. He made note of her description.

Chapter 23

February 11, 2111

The president's waiting room didn't impress Remus. He'd expected something grander. He jiggled his legs, unable to contain his excitement and nervousness. She was an hour late for their meeting, but he couldn't complain. Having an appointment was huge, and Remus didn't want to do anything to mess up his chance of getting his revenge on Pete. That bastard would pay for cutting him out of their pill business. Remus bumped something on the side table by this chair, then did a double take when he saw what was on it—a dish full of chocolate. He hadn't had it—or even seen any—in ten years. He grabbed a handful and stuffed them in his pockets for later. Part of his payment. The President could obviously afford if it was just sitting there for the taking.

The door to her office opened and her aide motioned for him to come in. He didn't bother to speak to Remus; instead he stood aside as Remus entered the room.

Remus couldn't believe he was standing in front of President Grieves. She was taller than he'd imagined. Older, too. His voice shook as he addressed her.

"Madame President."

President Grieves looked with disgust at the filthy little man.

"That title went out with the Dark Ages. Call me President Grieves." She went back to scrolling through her tablet. "Now get on with your report and stop wasting my time."

Remus's face became heated with embarrassment. "I apologize, I didn't know how to address you..." Remus bowed, and then changed his mind, which made him feel even stupider.

"President Grieves told you to stop wasting her time," said her aide. "I suggest you listen to her."

Remus wondered where Andrew was. He was the one who had assigned him the task of spying on Pete. This aide didn't appear to respect Remus at all.

"As I wrote in my report," he stammered, trying to control the shaking in his voice, "I found the Sleepers last night. They have a new member, a girl from the North Sector. Don't know her name, but will do my best to get that information for you if you think it's important, ma'am. That's why I needed to see you today instead of in two weeks, as we agreed upon."

"Doesn't matter, go on," she said, her voice sounding bored. "I have a busy schedule and can't spend all day listening to you."

"I overheard their leader, someone they call Decker. I'm not 100% sure about this, but everyone seems to defer to his decisions. He's suggesting they move their camp. Pretty sure that's happening soon. They're doing a lot of hunting and having long discussions."

"Can you lead us there?" asked President Grieves.

"Sure. I've gotten to know the area; it would be easy to sneak up on them. I've got a good hiding spot; they'll never know you're coming. I'm good in a fight, had plenty of practice."

"Then do whatever you need to do to get ready. I'll send a platoon of officers. You leave tomorrow afternoon."

"But what if they leave before then?"

"There are arrangements to be made first."

"President Grieves," he stammered. "I have more information for you."

"On with it!" she barked, causing Remus to flinch.

"The girl I told you about," said Remus, "I know she's not a Sleeper because I've seen her in line in the city getting assignments and sleeping pills. That's also how I figured out she was new to the group. Seems strange to me that she's living with them, unless she's pretending to need the pills. I just thought of that. Pretty smart, huh? I figured she could prove to be a good lead at some point."

Remus expected the President to look impressed. Instead she looked more irritated.

"Seems a bit shortsighted of you if she is a non-sleeper. She'll be dead soon enough. I've never seen anyone last longer than two weeks, so why would she be valuable to me? Or haven't you thought that scenario through?"

"Maybe she can tell us why she joined the Sleepers? Do you have any idea why?"

Remus looked stricken after realizing how disrespectful his statement sounded. His excitement over being a part of this operation had overruled his good sense. Panic rose in him.

"Pardon me, President Grieves, but I did mention to the police officers that I witnessed a robbery of Somnum sleeping pills," he said. "Perhaps that's how she's going to sleep. I saw the thief who broke into one of the pods. It was Pete Sanderson's pod. He was the reason I came to the police. It was their leader, Decker. I wondered what he was up to. Maybe that's the reason. What do you think?"

"What do I think?" she yelled. "As if a cretin such as yourself deserves to know what I think?"

Then President Grieves appeared to change her mind, and she bestowed one of her rare smiles to Remus. It gave him chills.

"This whole operation may become very interesting. You're dismissed. Collect your reward on the way out."

"Where should I meet the officers? I can be here at the assigned time or go wherever you want."

"You? I'm finished with you. Get out of my sight,

you little toad. No, you're a little rat, aren't you? Isn't that right? No, I've decided I don't need an amateur messing up things. Draw a map and leave it with my aide. We'll take it from here."

The aide smirked as he ushered Remus out. Remus left the President's office, furious at her dismissal of him. Like he was less than nothing. If he wanted to gain her respect, or at the very least, not be viewed as vermin, he needed more information. The raid was planned for tomorrow. He would go back to the Sleepers' encampment tonight and find out more about their plans. He was confident there was more information he could sell to the President, and this time she'd respect him.

He couldn't stand the idea of being nothing.

They watched Remus scurry away, a frightened rat pleased with himself for escaping from her wrath.

"President Grieves, may I ask you a question?" ventured her aide.

The President peered over the top of her glasses at him, irritated he'd disrupted her thoughts.

"What is it? Hurry up!" This aide was incompetent and much too nosy. She made a notation on her tablet to find a replacement.

"Why do you care about the Sleepers? They can't hurt us. I've never heard you discuss them before."

"By us I'm presuming you mean myself and my

cabinet. Don't assume to be important enough to understand the workings of this government. Now get out. You're dampening my mood."

Her aide looked stunned, his smirk from minutes ago gone. He lowered his head and left like a scolded puppy.

Glynis settled herself at her desk. She was preparing for her annual visit to Washington D.C. to plead her case. This would be the tenth time she'd ask the U. S. Government for permission to proceed with her plan.

Chapter 24

February 11, 2111

They were useless to her, and she was tired of being shackled to this pathetic city. A cure had been promised, but so far no one was successful.

She was so sick of it all. Ten years of babysitting a group of whiny citizens who contributed nothing to society. All the real work was done outside the borders of the Nation in the remaining parts of the United States. When she'd accepted this position, she thought it would be short term at best. At least, that's what the US president had insinuated. He'd seduced her with promises of power, the title of president of her own pseudo-country, and with the promise of being a part of his cabinet at a later date.

But that President had served his two terms, and now there was a new head of the United States. A younger man who seemed more ambitious than his predecessor. Last year, when she first met him, she knew there'd be trouble. Each year when she returned from her trek to Washington D.C., Glynis felt she was making progress. She'd prepared a compassionate—and she hoped convincing—speech about why there was no need to continue to support the non-sleepers. The first five years she was turned down with no chance for appeal. The main reason given: the unfairness of doing anything else to the hapless victims of an experiment gone wrong. Late in the term of the previous president, Jack Mosley, the man who had spearheaded the experiment, suggested to Glynis she was gaining ground in her argument. At that point, maintaining the Nation and its force was costing the United States millions of dollars. The money should be spent, in her opinion, on far more important things, and she wasn't alone in that opinion.

September 6, 2106
Five years AIB

"President Mosley, I've come to Washington D.C. every year for five years asking you to allow me to solve the problem of the non-sleepers. Year after year you have given me excuses about it being inhumane, how cruel it is, how this would look bad to the constituents. I changed my approach, hoping to use a different angle that you would understand, and still you did not approve. And now I'm appealing to your budgetary sense. Keeping the sleepless population in the Nation is costing the United States government millions of dollars per year, and for what? They contribute nothing. All they do is eat, defecate, procreate, and cost the taxpayers money. If the taxpayers knew you were throwing away all this money for nothing, how would they feel? You're in your second term, so maybe the constituents' happiness isn't an issue for you, but think of the other people in your party."

President Mosley remained silent, waiting for Glynis to go on.

"No comments, Jack? Has the great President Mosley finally lost his ability to speak? Or am I finally making sense to you?"

Glynis maintained unblinking eye contact with President Mosley. Daring him to disagree with her.

"Okay, Glynis, I think that the humanity angle on this has pretty much run its course. I agree about not wasting money, and so far no cure has been found. The thing is, if we move toward what you're planning, we need to do this in a way that no one else finds out. I propose we give the scientists a few more years to work on a cure. Wait before you interrupt me," he said, holding up his hand. "That way if anyone finds out about this it will look as if we tried to find a kinder solution. I can find the money to support the non-sleepers for a few more years. Once I leave office, I won't care about what you do. And maybe my replacement will be less of a humanitarian than I am."

Glynis fumed inwardly. Once again, he was

hedging. And now he was doing precisely what she'd feared he was going to do—leaving her high and dry.

Now, on her way to tomorrow's meeting, she was frustrated to be returning to D.C. yet again to get her solution approved. Glynis had prepared her best argument for when she was in front of the commission this year. She would threaten to tell the citizens of the Nation how they became sleepless and who was responsible. Until now it had never been discussed and no one in the Nation dared to ask her. And as far as the citizens in the rest of the United States were concerned, no one had survived the accident ten years ago. There was no real reason to suspect otherwise. The unaffected citizens in the U.S. were unaware what the infection did to people, and no one was willing to risk going into the quarantine area.

That was why the CDC put up the Garbage Wall around the area and the fact that no one who entered the Nation on the day of the disaster was ever seen outside of that area again. Those living outside the Wall thought it was built to keep anyone from entering the infected area. No one could have guessed it was to keep the sleepless from escaping. Glynis knew if she disclosed the truth—that there were thousands of sleepless survivors—the new president's administration would unravel. There was also a chance the previous administration would be brought up on charges.

Glynis smiled. She couldn't wait to see the look of shock and fear in the faces of the President and the head of the CDC. They wouldn't be able to say no to her this time.

Chapter 25

February 10, 2111

At the evening fire, Kate surprised Decker by standing up and giving a speech out of concern for her new community, and somehow she convinced them they were in danger. She confirmed their fears about Sleepers disappearing. New signs appeared in the city in the last month asking the citizens to call the government if they knew of any Sleepers. It was worded to sound as if the government wanted to study the Sleepers to find a cure. Kate didn't believe this and told her new friends of her suspicions.

The Sleepers then discussed Kate's concerns at length and decided they would pack up and leave the next morning. It would be the last time this group sat around that particular campfire, a home they'd known for almost two years. Prior to this place, they'd moved around every two to three months in the wooded areas of the North Sector, to prevent discovery.

This is the right decision, thought Decker, but he was surprised by his sadness. The whole situation was messed up. He needed to know why the world stopped sleeping. There had to be a way to cure it. One of his goals when they left this place was to search beyond the North Sector; he had hopes they could find the other Sleepers Bridget mentioned. It was difficult for Decker to believe there was no life beyond the Nation. He'd seen birds flying past the Wall, which meant plants and small animals must have survived the plague.

And yet Decker knew he needed to keep the Sleepers, his adopted family, safe. He would lead them farther north hoping to find another oasis for them to live in.

"Decker?" said Kate. "You're not mad that I talked the group into moving, are you? I thought I needed to speak up. I've lived in the North City and know President Grieves wouldn't hesitate to have you all executed if she thought you were trying to upset things."

"Don't worry, Kate, I'm glad you spoke up. And you're right; we do need to leave. You're braver than me, Katie girl. Besides, I'm ready to leave our little campsite; we've stayed in one place too long. There's something better out there, I know it."

Rustling in the trees startled Kate and Decker. They turned and saw a shadow standing just past the tree line. Kate stepped in front of Decker and yelled to determine if it was an animal or a person.

"Identify yourself! Who's there?"

No answer. She yelled even louder, "Who goes there? Make yourself known!"

A young man stepped out from behind the trees and walked toward them.

"Stop!" warned Kate. "I asked you to identify yourself, and while you're at it, what are you doing here?"

"It's okay," said Decker. "I know this guy. He's the one from the arena. The one who watched me clean and promised not to say anything." He turned to him. "Aidan, right?"

"Yeah, you're the guy who cleans," said Aidan. "So this is your friend? The one I saw you with that day?"

"Yep," said Decker. Then he squinted at him. "How did you find us? You're not here to cause trouble, are you?"

Aidan shoved his hands in his pockets. "No, I don't want any trouble. I'm here to help and maybe get some help in return. I had to leave, man. I can't stay in the city any longer. I saw you on the ITS and followed you here."

Decker and Kate looked at each other. Decker knew if Aidan could follow him here, anyone could. A worrisome thought.

"I have no idea who you are but you seemed like a decent guy. The fact that you were willing to do a cleanup for someone else convinced me you were good. I hope I'm not mistaken."

"Well, I'm Decker, and this is Kate. If you call her anything else, she'll smack you."

"Nice to meet you, Kate."

Kate gave Aidan a brief nod. Decker could tell she was thinking about Ling and Jordan because her eyes were filling with tears. An awkward silence grew. At last, she said, "I hate to ask, but I'm sure you understand. We really need to know why you're running away."

Decker nodded in agreement.

Aidan's face shut down, the smile was gone, the cockiness disappeared.

"Because I looked into the eyes of two people I didn't know, and I killed them. And for what? For sleeping pills? No, I'm done. I've only got enough to last me a few weeks, but I figure I can do *something* to make up for what I did in that time."

Decker couldn't help but smile. "I've got good news for you on that front," he said. "We have a stash of sleeping pills both you and Kate can use."

Claudia walked up to the three of them. "I think that before we can allow Aidan to join our group, he needs to prove himself."

Aidan sat down on a nearby rock to listen to the group discuss his future. Decker sent him there knowing there was nothing else Aidan could do to convince them. The Sleepers had a decision to make.

"Jeremy, what do you think?" said Decker. "Do you agree that we need some way to prove that Aidan isn't a spy?"

Jeremy walked to this center of the circle, addressing Claudia and the rest of them.

"Yes, I agree we need to do something, and I have no clue what. What kind of tests could he be put through? Maybe a challenge of some sort? And it needs to happen right away. We've already decided on the urgent need to move from here."

Decker watched Kate stand up and address the group of Sleepers.

"Why don't you trust him? It would have been easy for him to report on Decker doing my cleaning. But he chose to keep his promise and stay silent. Instead, he came here on his own, putting himself in danger; he's been through a struggle. None of us have ever had to kill a person, so I'm not sure why you don't trust Aidan."

The group erupted in conversation. Decker walked in the middle of the circle and motioned for everyone to be quiet.

"Look, I know we're all scared, but my inclination is to agree with the majority here. I would like to trust him"—he nods in the direction of Aidan—"but it's too important to the group to maintain our safety. So yes, I think we need to figure out some sort of challenge. But first let's put it to a vote. If you think we should just accept Aidan without a challenge, put a black stone into the bag. If you think he needs to prove himself in some way, vote with a white stone."

Each Sleeper was given one black and one white stone and told to return in five minutes after they contemplated their answers. Aidan looked worried as he watched the group walk off in several directions. Some alone, others in pairs, all deciding his fate. Decker nodded to indicate Kate should hold the voting bag.

"Since Kate's the newest member, she can be the one to count out the stones."

"Okay, so do I just dump them out on the stump? What's the best way to handle this?" said Kate, looking at the Sleepers.

Jeremy walked over to her. "However you want to handle this is fine. We need to get the final vote and move on."

Kate emptied the bag onto one of the stumps that served as a table for the community. She didn't take long to get the results. In front of her: four black stones and twenty white ones. They'd decided. Aidan needed to perform some type of challenge to prove himself.

"I've been thinking about it. The task that we're going to assign to Aidan should be something to prove his trustworthiness and also helps us as a community. Given these parameters, the best thing for him to do is to go back into North City and steal some seeds from two of the farms. When we leave the encampment, we're going to need to continue to be a self-sustaining unit. One of the things essential to that is for us to be able to grow our own vegetables after we've established ourselves elsewhere."

Decker looked around at the gathered Sleepers,

trying to read their faces. They were overwhelmingly in favor of Aidan proving himself, so Decker felt fairly confident his suggestion would be accepted.

Kate returned to the center and spoke up.

"I do agree with Decker. I think if he is willing to go back to the city and do this, that will be proof enough for me. Anyone else agree?"

Everyone's hand went up. Several of the Sleepers were nodding.

Kate remained in the center and waited until everyone quieted down. "He can't go alone to do this, so who amongst us will volunteer to go along with him? I know that I'm willing, but I don't know anything about farming and would not be a good candidate for identifying the right seeds for us." She returned to her seat and waited for someone to speak up.

Jeremy spoke next.

"I'm not an expert, but I can identify plants and know enough to keep them alive."

The group looked pleased that Jeremy would go with Aidan.

"All that's left is to find out if Aidan is willing to perform this for us."

"Yes, absolutely!" he yelled. "I want to get away, and if this is what it takes, then so be it. When would you like me to go?"

"Early in the morning," said Decker. "We all thank Jeremy for helping out. There should be more than enough time to get there and come back before anyone in the city notices the missing seeds and plants. Part of Jeremy's duty will be to ensure Aidan doesn't lead anyone back here. Sorry, Aidan, but until this is over, I can't give you my complete trust."

"I hope this works out," said Jeremy, moving in closer to Decker so Aidan couldn't hear. "My gut still tells me he's a good kid."

Chapter 26

February 11, 2111

It was an unsettling feeling to Aidan, knowing he had no control over the situation. His only consolation at this point was that he could return to North City, and since he had told no one he was leaving, there would be no repercussions. There was a good chance his absence hadn't been noticed. But he really wanted to stay with this group. Once the Sleepers voted to give him a chance, he felt a small measure of relief.

Aidan looked down at the list of vegetable and fruit seeds Decker wanted him to steal. Carrot, Beet, Potato, Strawberry, Raspberry, Blackberry.

Fruit and vegetables grew on separate farms, so Aidan would have to steal from two different places, increasing their chances of getting caught. Then he realized it was his chance of getting caught that increased, not Jeremy's. Jeremy was coming along to keep an eye on him and wouldn't be part of the pilfering. The vegetables would be easier—all he had to do was find the planting shed and grab the seeds.

Aidan dreaded going to the fruit farm. He'd have to dig up young plants to take with him.

"Do you know anything about farming, Aidan?" Jeremy asked, interrupting his thoughts.

"No, not really. My mother had an herb garden in our backyard BIB, but I was a little kid then with no interest in growing anything. I was more interested in collecting baseball cards. What about you?"

"I had a small plot in a community garden in Chicago. Grew peas, tomatoes, and strawberries. Thought it was relaxing after a day working in tech. My job was interesting but stressful. I used to build hardware. You know, things like computers and the occasional robot for fun."

"Good, you can help me identify the plants and seeds we need."

"Don't forget, I'm not going into the farms with you, but you can show me what you get, and if it's not right, you can go back."

The closer they got to the farms, the more Aidan felt anxious. He'd never stolen anything before, never been in any trouble. This would be crossing a line for him. Then he realized how ridiculous his feelings were, considering he had recently killed two innocent people. Stealing was a lot further down the list of bad things than killing was. He laughed out loud.

"What's so funny, dude?" asked Jeremy.

"I was thinking about what I'm about to do. Feeling bad about stealing, then it dawned on me I'm a killer. Pretty ridiculous, right?"

Jeremy stopped walking and stared at Aidan.

"Seriously, dude, you need to get over that. You did what you had to do. And now you're doing something else that's necessary. You're about to prove yourself to the rest of us." He gave him a sideways glance, then added, "With the *fruits* of your labor."

They both laughed.

"Seriously, though, this will help feed us, to sustain us. So when you think about it, stealing, at least in this case, is a good thing."

Aidan nodded. Jeremy was a good guy. He hoped he passed this test, because he could see himself becoming friends with him.

"Okay, it looks like were about a quarter-mile from the fruit farm. How close are you going to get, Jeremy?"

"I need to be close enough to watch you in case you get in trouble, but not so close that if you get caught, they discover me."

Aidan turned to look at Jeremy.

"Sorry," said Jeremy, holding his hands up. "I know that sounds harsh, but you're the one that's supposed to be stealing. I'm just an observer. So I'm thinking I'll find a building, a tree, something that I can hide behind. Let's keep going, I'll know it when I see it."

Next to the fence was a discarded rusty tractor. Aidan pointed it out to Jeremy.

"That would be a good place for you to hide, underneath the tractor, as long as you don't mind getting dirty. And I should be in your sight most of the time. Do we have a signal so you can let me know if you see anyone coming? I don't expect you to rescue me, but it would be nice to get some warning before I get ambushed."

"How about a whistle? Like this." Jeremy slid his little fingers into both sides of his mouth, pursed his lips, and blew an ear-piercing whistle.

"Yeah, that'll do. That's loud enough to warn the whole city."

"Okay, I'll tone it down a little."

Once Jeremy got settled under the tractor, Aidan proceeded to the fruit farm. Trying to calm his nerves, Aidan focused on his task. Looking at the map Decker drew, Aidan spotted the shed on the fruit farm. Drawn on the map were sketches of raspberry and blackberry bushes, to help him identify which ones to dig up. He spotted some near the tool shed.

Decker had told him the shed should be unlocked, and it was, much to Aidan's relief. He opened the door with caution, paranoid there might be an alarm of some sort. He knew he was being irrational, but couldn't help it. Being successful was important to him; he needed nothing getting in his way.

Aidan grabbed a trowel from the shed then returned to the outside to dig up blackberry and raspberry bushes. Decker wanted five of each type. While walking there, Jeremy had told him to be sure to get the entire root ball, and then he had to explain what a root ball was. He also needed to include a portion of dirt to keep the roots moist. The soil was loose, which allowed Aidan to dig up the plants with little effort. He put them in the bag he was carrying and went back inside the shed. From one shelf, he grabbed a handful of strawberry seeds and deposited them in a small cloth bag and placed them inside with the plants. He peered outside to check to if anyone was around and saw he was still alone. Happy that the first part of his mission was going smoothly, he made his way back to Jeremy and told him he could come out from under the tractor.

"Well, that's one down, one to go, Jeremy."

Aidan felt more confident than he had earlier in the day. Perhaps this would work out. He hoped so. He didn't want to run into anyone, and he especially didn't want to fight. Fighting was behind him. Aidan never wanted to do that again. They walked in amiable silence the short distance to the vegetable farm. This time Jeremy hid behind a nearby bush. Aidan continued on to the farm and repeated what he'd done earlier. There were shelves and shelves of vegetable seeds and he felt nervous, not really sure which ones to take. The shelves weren't marked, so this would be a guessing game for him. The tiny sketches of the seeds drawn by Decker weren't useful in the dim light of the shed. He didn't want to return if he chose the wrong ones. Aidan decided on the spot, he would grab a handful of each one, and once he returned to the encampment, Decker could decide which ones to keep and which ones to throw away. As he is about to leave the shed, he heard someone walking past.

Oh shit, oh shit. Now what?

Aidan snuck a look out of one of the windows and watched an old man standing a few feet from the shed with a rake in his hand. The man paused for a moment as if listening. Aidan held his breath, willing himself not to move. A moment later the man moved on. Relief at not being discovered unfroze his body. As soon as the man was out of sight, Aidan ran to Jeremy's hiding spot.

"That was close!" said Aidan.

"I know, I was trying to decide how to rescue you."

"Well, I'm not sure that guy could have caught me."

They both laughed, relieved.

"Hey, while we're in the city, is there anything else we should get?" asked Aidan. "I'm already a thief, maybe I should use my new skill."

"Try not to get carried away. I think you've stolen enough for one day, dude. Let's head home."

"Oh, come on. You could all use some new clothes. Some of you look like you've been wearing the same stuff for years. Let me grab some stuff on our way out."

Aidan made a compelling argument. He'd observed the threadbare clothing and shoes with thin soles.

"Let's say I agree with you. How would we do it?"

"We?"

Jeremy sighed. "If we're getting clothes, you can't do it on your own. Plus, I don't know if I want you choosing what I get to wear for the next five years."

Aidan laughed. "All right, well, it seems the doors in this city aren't locked. Shall we just go to the back door of the clothing factory and see what we can grab? If anyone is there, we'll say we got lost."

"Man, I know I'm going to regret this. Okay, let's do it."

The nearest clothing factory was by the main ITS station, making for a quick getaway. They tried the back door, and sure enough, it was unlocked.

"I'll scope it out, Aidan, you've done enough stealing today. Watch the door and I'll grab what I can. I should only be two or three minutes."

Once Jeremy disappeared into the factory, Aidan felt worried. He didn't want his new friend to get caught.

Jeremy reappeared minutes later. "Time to get out of here! I don't think anyone heard me. Hurry to the station! I'll show you what I got on the train."

Jeremy looked flushed with excitement. They were heading home with more than they'd planned on. The Sleepers would be thrilled with both of them.

Home. Aidan liked the sound of that. If he couldn't return to his biological family, the Sleepers would become his new family.

Chapter 27

February 12, 2111

In the space of twenty-four hours, their number had grown by two. They now numbered thirty, including the children. All looking for a better life, and two searching for a cure for their sleeplessness. Decker had heard rumors of a hidden door in the wall of garbage, but until he found it, he didn't want to tell the rest of the group. False hope wasn't a good thing. He wanted to keep the Sleepers hopeful but not fixated on one solution. If the door was fiction, Decker needed to think of another way to get out of the Nation.

Aidan walked up to him, watching everyone pack up and get things ready for today's journey.

"Hey, Aidan," said Claudia, "since you have nothing to pack, would you help with taking down the tents?"

"Sure thing. I think I can figure it out. Never camped or gardened, but I've gotta learn sometime. Do you mind if I distribute the new clothes Jeremy and I got first?"

"Sure, but be quick about it."

The Sleepers gathered around the young Santa Clauses, waiting to see what they'd receive. Everyone had something new. Pants, shirts, and best of all: boots. There was disappointment about the lack of any new jackets; they'd have to layer to keep warm. It was tough carrying a huge load of goods from the factory to the encampment, but between the two of them, they'd managed.

Decker enjoyed seeing Aidan help, trying to fit in. He knew Aidan's missing digit hindered him and felt a twinge of guilt about incinerating the finger. The technology needed to reattach it had disappeared AIB. No one with the skill or equipment for such an operation lived in the Nation.

"Hey, Decker, we have a special present for you." Jeremy pulled out a new pair of boots for him. "I know you like to run and will miss your shoes, but man they are falling off your feet. You can learn to run in these boots. Soldiers do it all the time."

Decker was touched by their kindness and tried the boots on right away.

"Thanks, guys. I was concerned about walking for untold miles with what was left of my running shoes. These fit great."

Just past 8 AM, they were ready. The Sleepers cleaned up their campsite, then slipped on backpacks and began their trek north. Unaware Decker was searching for something specific, they were happy to follow their leader. Jeremy, the last person to leave the encampment, was instructed by Decker to perform a final sweep of the area so it looked as if no one had ever been there. The fire pit was filled in, footprints were swept away, and no garbage was left behind.

The morning was cool but there was no sign of snow. Leaving at this time of year worried the group because they weren't well equipped for cold weather. During the previous winters they could survive by staying close to their encampment, staying in their tents, and building fires. They were limited to the clothing they brought with them from their BIB lives and the new ones they'd gotten from Jeremy and Aidan. Because they'd been forced to pack in haste and could not bring much with them, they all lacked enough heavy clothes to get them through any kind of severe snowstorm. The subject of skinning the animals they caught for food and making coats and boots was broached, but no one in their group had the skill.

"Decker, where are we heading?" asked Kate.

"I've been thinking about it," said Decker, "and I think we need to continue heading north. I haven't told the rest the group yet, but during my visits into North City I overheard people talking about a rumor of a door in the Wall. Once we reach the Wall, we'll head west and search for both an exit and the other Sleepers."

Kate stopped walking.

"Kate, keep going," he whispered. "I don't want

anyone else to know what we're talking about."

"Tell me more about this door."

"The rumor is there is a door built somewhere into the Wall and that's how the equipment that the President and her government uses is transported. It makes sense because whenever I've seen her, she always looks like she has on a new suit. Nothing about her government looks worn out, nothing looks ten years old like everything in here. There has to be a way for them to be obtaining supplies. But if that's the case, then what exactly is beyond the Wall?"

"But, Decker, you need to tell the rest the group about this. Whether it's true or not, they all deserve to know what you're looking for and where we're headed. I know that I'd be pissed off at you if you were withholding this from me. Can you imagine how the rest of them, who have lived with you for years, are going to feel?"

Decker considered this and almost regretted telling any of it to Kate. But in a way he was glad because she had good sense and the ability to read other people. In the two days the Sleepers had known her, they'd all accepted her and were happy to have her among them. She was right. After they set up camp that evening, he would gather them and tell them what he knew, or at least what he suspected.

"Okay, you're right, Kate, but can it wait until tonight? And then we can all have a discussion and go from there."

Decker felt a tap on his shoulder and turned around. It was Bridget. Although she was in her early sixties, she was as fit as anyone else in the group and was lugging a backpack as large as his.

"Decker, is there anything else I can do for the group? You have been so generous to me. You and the Sleepers took me in, and you gave me back my granddaughter. There has to be something else I can do."

Decker saw Kate smile and knew she was still amazed the two of them had been reunited.

"If I think of something, I'll let you know. Are there any special skills I should know about? You already help with cooking and mending clothes. Is there something else you can do that would be of use to all of us?"

Bridget's eyes twinkled. "I'm sure Kate remembers the stories I used to tell her about hiking the Pacific Crest Trail years ago. I was in my forties then. The trail is something like 2,700 miles."

"Yes, you've mentioned it, Bridget."

"Well, yes, I used to be pretty outdoorsy. Being on my own these last ten years, I've put a lot of miles on my old legs and they're still holding up. Anyway, my point is, Decker, I'm an expert at orienteering. I have a great sense of direction, can build a fire the old-fashioned way, and can construct a shelter with a few sticks and leaves."

"Good to know, Bridget. We may be relying on

your skill set soon. For now let's enjoy this gorgeous day and keep heading north."

Remus could tell none of them knew he was trailing them. Watching them from afar and hiding behind trees the previous evening. He'd spent the night in a nearby cave and almost missed the Sleepers leaving. President Grieves hadn't given him the respect he thought he deserved. Perhaps if he found out where they were going, she'd let him help with their capture. He considered joining them and spying from within the group. Maybe later. He needed to learn more about the group dynamics.

After that, he'd find a way to fool them all.

"Hold on everyone, I hear something," said Decker.

No one moved, tense with anticipation. An older, grizzled man stepped out from the bushes, attempting a smile. Decker recognized him as the person he'd ditched while setting up the fake buy for Somnum.

They needed to be cautious.

"Hello, you're Remus, right? Hey, I'm sorry I didn't show up for our meeting. I got delayed."

"You never intended to meet up with me, did you, boy?"

"I did, Remus."

Remus shook his head and spat on the ground.

"I've told the president about all of you. A group of soldiers is coming to raid your camp today. When they discover you've already left, they'll come after you. There is no escape."

His smile turned into a sneer.

"Why would you do that to us?" asked Kate.

"You should know, missy. It's because *they* can sleep and I can't. It's not fair. I hate them stinking Sleepers! If I can't sleep, why should they?"

Jeremy moved closer to Remus. Decker hoped Remus wouldn't notice, and he spoke up to distract him.

"But, Remus, hating us for something we can't help makes no sense. That's like saying you hate me because I have blond hair."

Before Remus could reply, Jeremy tackled him to the ground.

"What the hell are you doing? Get off me!"

"You can't just come here and threaten all of us like that," said Jeremy, finally getting a firm grip on Remus's arms.

The Sleepers were getting agitated. Decker had taught his group to be non-violent, but their survival was at stake. Now he needed to step up and try to fix this.

Kate must have had the same idea because she spoke before Decker could.

"Remus, I don't resent the Sleepers; I'm happy for them. You should direct your hate toward the

President and her government. Haven't you ever wanted to leave North City?"

Remus struggled against Jeremy's hold and glared up at Kate. "Why should I? There isn't anywhere to go. You'll find that out if you keep running."

"You only say that because you believe what they tell you. When did you lose the ability to think for yourself? Why don't you join us? Do you really think you'll get a reward for turning us in?"

"What? Don't invite this scumbag to join us," said Jeremy.

Remus appeared to be thinking about Kate's remarks. The rest of the Sleepers were moving away from him, getting ready to run.

Remus struggled again, then went limp. "Why would you invite me? You can't bait me, missy. Give me a reason to join your bunch."

"Hope, Remus. Maybe there's a cure, or maybe not. We want to find out. Decide now. If there are soldiers looking for us, there's no more time to debate this."

Decker stepped between Kate and Remus.

"She's right, Remus. Decide now, or we'll tie your hands and feet and dump you in the bushes. The soldiers might find you. But I'm guessing you'll never be discovered and die of exposure."

The rest of the Sleepers walked away. Jeremy continued to hold Remus, waiting for direction from Decker.

Decker growled in frustration. "Damn it, you're giving us little choice here."

Decker reached into his backpack and pulled out a rope.

"Tie his hands in front of him and leave enough rope for one of us to lead him."

"Then what?"

"We can't trust him. Until he earns our trust, we take him with us then leave him once we're far enough into the forest for him to get lost."

Decker frowned. Making tough decisions was the part of leadership he hated. Jeremy finished tying Remus up.

"Okay, let's get moving."

Kate, Aidan, and the Sleepers continued their hike away from their home toward a new life full of unknowns. All but Remus dared to hope for a better future.

Chapter 28

February 12, 2111

After the introductions to the committee members, President Glynis Grieves sat down. Today was the day that would change the course of her future and that of the sleepless. She'd spent the last month preparing her speech.

"President Grieves," said Chairman Stevens, "we are ready for your testimony about the Nation. Everyone in this room knows the backstory so there is no need to go over how we got to this point. All we want to hear from you is what you propose to do about it."

Glynis cleared her throat, ready to give a performance none of these politicians would forget.

"Chairman Stevens, Honorable Senators, and other members of this esteemed committee, I come before you today as I have for the last ten years with what I consider a humanitarian request. I've spent this last decade caring for the unfortunate souls forever changed by the aftereffects of an experiment gone wrong. If you remember, an experiment approved by all of you. You asked me not to go over how we got here, but my testimony wouldn't be complete without at least a short summary. Your memories and your consciences need to be nudged to help you make the right decision this time. We were entering another era of a difficult relationship with Russia and all of you felt we needed to come up with a weapon to protect our great country. Nuclear weapons weren't enough because there were those among you who believed that neither side would use them. And yet, not having a way to control our enemy was a threat to our sense of security and for our place in the world. I was at that first meeting when we discussed the development of a biological weapon to subdue our enemies."

Chairman Stevens looked irritated.

"What's your point, Glynis? We know this. Please go on with your new testimony."

"I won't be silenced, Jeff." She loved throwing him off his game by using his first name. "You need to hear everything I am saying."

Chairman Stevens sat back and motioned for her to continue.

"I trust that will be the last interruption from any of you," she continued with disdain. "The purpose of this weapon was to make the leaders of the country docile and non-threatening. An antidote for testosterone poisoning, as I call it." She smiled at her joke. "The target was the president, prime minister, and all who worked in the Duma and the Federal Assembly of Russia. No innocents to be infected. That's what this committee said. But then some of you got cold feet. 'Let's test it,' you said. After a few days of discussion, you gave your approval to the director of the CDC. It was decided a test of the virus would be performed in Chicago. Go to the prison there and dose the most dangerous felons. It didn't matter to any of you that an antidote wasn't ready yet. These were a bunch of hoods that didn't deserve to be free. So what happened? We still don't know who put the virus into the water supply. Wait, let me correct that statement. *I* still don't know who put the virus in the water supply."

Glynis stopped to fill her glass and sip her water.

"Let's hope my glass of water isn't contaminated, gentlemen. As soon as the error was discovered, pandemonium ensued, and I was left to deal with all of it. That brings us to today. Today the Nation is filled with a population you'd like to forget about. The casualties of your paranoia, your false bravado. Every day my citizens face a future of sleeplessness. I've tried to keep them engaged by creating the Sector Series, and I'm happy to say it's largely a success. It's as popular as the Super Bowl. But for that entertainment, I know the people living there are on the verge of rising up against me and trying to overthrow everything I've built. But, gentlemen, I am tired. Tired of keeping these non-sleepers going. They contribute nothing. All they do is consume. I'm not even allowed to sterilize them, so they keep having babies. Every baby born is another sleepless citizen of the Nation. It's time for you, for us, to do the right thing. Put these people out of their misery. Let me finally euthanize the population. I'm not a monster, but I cannot go on supporting an unnatural way of life. They are a nation of abominations."

The committee members looked at one another in shock and horror.

"Before you consider how to word denying my request, let me explain one more thing to you. You will give me the permission I'm seeking this time. If, when I return tomorrow, my request has been denied, then I go public. I've documented everything about your great experiment and am prepared to release this information to the world. Imagine what will happen when all is revealed. You will be labeled monsters and most, if not all of you, will be prosecuted for the use of illegal biological warfare upon your own citizens."

Glynis stood up, picking up her tablet.

"Right before I stepped into this hearing, I was informed a group of Sleepers escaped from North City today and were last seen heading toward the Wall. Do you really want them to find out about all of this? I leave it to you to make the right decision. I'll be back in the morning to find out if you are indeed among the most intelligent men in the country or whether all these years sitting on your behinds has only made you soft."

The committee watched Glynis Grieves leave the room. No one spoke.

Dr. Annie Beaumont was reeling. President Grieves' testimony had horrified her. Annie knew this was the agenda the last president had tried to get approval on for both of his terms. This time Grieves might get her way and have the sleepless euthanized. She needed to get back to her lab at the CDC and talk to her manager about increased funding. The need for a cure for the sleepless was more urgent than ever. She didn't want the mass murder of thousands of people on her conscience.

This disaster was partly her fault. Her salvation rested on her ability to fix it.

The End

Acknowledgements

To Crystal Watanabe my patient editor, thank you for helping me find the right words.

To my pillow, for saving me from the nightmare of insomnia.

ABOUT THE AUTHOR

I have been scribbling stories since I was a child and love to write Science Fiction, Magical Realism, and Modern Gothic. Many writers like to specialize but I enjoy mixing it up and exploring different genres.

My first memory of Science Fiction was watching the television show, "The Twilight Zone". That series messed with my mind! My imagination developed, helping me discover the lack of conventional boundaries in storytelling. Because my fiction is character driven, the focus of my stories tends to be about emotions, relationships, and society.

I live in the Pacific Northwest with my greatest fans: my husband Mark, twin sons Aidan and Jared, and four cats. When not writing, I love to travel, run, use the Oxford comma, and of course read!

Thank you for taking the time to read *The Sleepless*. If you enjoyed it, please consider posting a short review. Cheers!

Please visit my website to find out more about my books: www.dkcassidy.com

www.ingramcontent.com/pod-product-compliance
Lightning Source LLC
Chambersburg PA
CBHW071510170626
46811CB00007B/2799